The Man
Who Noticed
Everything

Contents

For Darcy, who allows me to notice—
and who herself never fails to notice everything

The Man
Who Noticed
Everything

Hard Water

The frost on the windowpane is thinner. I begin to notice figures on the road again. Not in droves but one by one, coming on slow as the springtime. From where I sit above the road, in an old wicker chair at my bedroom window, the destinations of the figures, simply put, are not mine, and I don't tend to wonder past what I can see. Country trash in battered traps, a tinker with a burlap sack full of lightning rods, occasionally my neighbor, Penderton, a cotton-man, or one of his sulking negro boys on his way to the sundry or still for provisions, not that it is any of my business.

I am mostly in the habit of watching these days.

Even the traveling medicine show, with its slim, murky vials and malformed proprietor, interests me no further than the filthy wagon tarp, the swelling clatter of the wheels, the snuffle of horses gone by me.

When I think of the lip of the world, and I do, I'm thinking of my own front yard.

Every so often, I see the boy. Not that I am watching for him. He walks with his satchel at his hip up the parallax of birches that lines the dirt road. He walks in a way that his left arm swings free, as though with a mind to be elsewhere. Sometimes he stops just in front of my gate to blow back the hair from in front of his eyes, or to pivot the weight of his satchel behind him, and having done so walks on. Once I even called his name. Benjamin, I said, it is me, Colby Marshall. But he did not seem to hear my voice, or maybe I spoke too quiet.

When I am not at the window, I tend to my plants. It is small, steady work, and belabors the nerves. These are vital hours for my crop of White Burley, if they are to make it to hogshead come summer. The leaves are yellowing in their beds, peeping hello above the edges. My hands shake a little in the gloom of the barn as inch by inch I trim them green. As for the fields, they are fallow and scentless. Sometimes in the morning, or before the sun drops, a limbo of fog from the mountains hangs over them, and lends the earth an untold depth.

In the evenings, when the traffic on the road thins out and I have done all that I can for the plants, I sit in my parlor and read the book. Don Juan, it is called, by Lord Byron. I have other books, too, nigh a whole parlor full, propped spine to spine along rude wooden shelves, some of them come from as near as Atlanta when I go there to meet with distributing agents, others as far as San Francisco, delivered by post, after weeks. Entertainments by Stevenson and Defoe, who big city readers might label as common, illumine no less my place in the world than the sublime compositions of Wordsworth or Shelley, not that I put much stock in the words of those who do not do. And unlike most who take their ease on a chilly spring night with a book, as I do, I sip PG Tips instead of spirits, which I have found augments perception. This rare leaf makes it way to my crockery across the Atlantic every month; with it come soaps, water crackers, cologne and a case of Bordeaux I will save for the harvest. Byron's epic poem was a gift from the boy so I might better grasp his leaving; every spring for three years, I have read it afresh, so I might grasp, in turn, some comfort. But this spring I am no closer than I was the last, nor was I the last than the spring before that. And so it continues on and on.

I fear before long I will have it to memory.

In the portraits I've found of Lord Byron himself, I recognize particles of the boy. Byron, of course, is the boy gone to pot from the excess of his later years, but the pitiless beauty of his face suggests, in good light, a former softness. If the boy was anything, he was soft. I could have balled him in my hand. And wherever he is, be it Spain or Greece, at the mouth of the Danube or waist-coated London, I hope he has retained his softness, and yet cultivates it for me, his friend. At present, I am groping through Canto V, when Don Juan finds himself on the Turkish slave market.

The irony is not lost on me that shackles do not make the slave.

It is getting on toward April when I see the drifter coming. I know he is a drifter for he drifts, though on horseback, sloughing side to side across the withers of his mount. The horse is little better than a nag, journey-eaten. Though it feels early yet for the plague of blow-flies that descends on these parts with the first of the heat, the nag shakes its head and bares its teeth with the old agony of a darling. From my window, the rider's face is hidden. His hat brim hangs over his face like a caul. He reigns up his horse at the gate to my house, a modest one, if that. I live alone. A galleried porch with a screen door behind it, whose keeper spring cackles as I come through, is mirrored by a second story tier right above it, better painted than the first, like a stale wedding cake.

By the time I am off the front porch, moving toward him, he has dropped from his mount and is wiping his face. He wipes it with the hat brim that formerly hid it, a long, sponging motion from brow to chin, and having achieved, then, an optimal dryness, wrings it out in the dirt, sets it back on his head. Despite the mild air, he is covered in sweat, as though he'd been riding for miles at a gallop.

Fine morning, he says, though it is noon. I'd ask if you might have some work that needs doing.

None I haven't got a start on.

Well, says the man, as he hitches his trousers. Well, he says again. He squints.

He is powerfully built I can see now I'm nearer, in a dirty white smock unlaced to his sternum. Save for the straight line of his jaw, muzzled with a few days' beard, there is a strange asymmetry to his features that is hard to pinpoint from the place I am standing. The face is not ugly, or even unlovely, with its leading man's lips and denuding bright eyes, but then, drawing closer, it's the eyes above all that I bring to account for the face's keel, for lo one is set higher up than the other, like a portrait warped by damp.

Been riding since Macon, hang sleep or a meal. I wouldn't tell either to shoo, if you'll have me.

I'm not for handing out, I say.

Well, he repeats, with incantatory slowness. Folks is got their own philosophy.

I lean on the gatepost, which ventures a creak. I have kept my eyes on him a moment too long.

Macon's not so far from here.

On this here maggot trap it is. He slaps the nag's flank and it grumbles a pace. Ain't that right, John Wilkes? he croons.

I run the place myself, I say. Good morning to you all the same, and I turn, but then I hear him crossing the road in my direction. Wait up, friend, he calls. Whoa there.

I turn to find him standing on the crossbeam of the gate with his elbows hunched over the top. He waves me over.

I could do other things for you too, I expect. Just a man getting on with no wife, by hisself.

No thank you, I say. You heard me the first time.

Sure, he says. You run it yournself. No pies in the windows that I can make out. But hey, he waves me closer, I'm telling you now. We could squeeze one off later on, if you like.

For a scorched, airless moment, I can only stare at him. The touch of another, no matter how light, has pummeled me once and then twice in the face. I see that his eyes are not only uneven, but different colors altogether; the right one, set higher, is pearlescent and grey, while the left, more or less where an eye should reside, has a rheumy, washed-out bluish tint, like a thimble of cheap cologne.

What's your name? I ask him then.

V, he says.

The letter? I ask.

Twenty-second of its kind.

Though I know it matters little, I take in the road. A breeze stalks the trees, on a wag or a beckon, but other than that it is empty and still.

I nod to V's horse: You can tie him out back.

Didn't catch your name there, friend.

He is still hanging over the gate, staring at me.

Beg pardon, he says to my back, and comes on.

I watch over V while he hitches John Wilkes to a muscular tree in my back yard. As soon as he's knotted the reins at the trunk—a fisherman's knot, I note, what kind?—its shabby knees buckle and fold in the dirt and its head cradles onto its forelegs. It is a pitiful creature, befitting its rider, who seems to see it more as a friend than a horse. Though I should wonder from its carriage and the scarlands of its flanks if the friendship they share is reciprocal.

Set tight, there, John Wilkes, says V. Dream a little while while I'm gone.

The horse grumbles.

So what all did you have in mind? he says, looking at me, framed against my empty fields.

The rows need turning, I say. Groundwork. I'll fetch you a harrow directly.

Ain't you got a team for all that? he says. Or is you still hitching up niggers?

No, no team, I say. Too expensive. I run the place myself, remember?

I ain't forgot what you told me, he says. And I got elbow grease to burn.

I leave him there braced at the edge of the field while I go to the shed to retrieve him a harrow. In the gloom the farm tools have a sinister look, like the cutlery of a giant.

When I come with the harrow pitched over my shoulder, V is still beneath the tree. Aside from that tree, my lone water tower and the jumble of Penderton's distant spread, he and his horse are the sole occupants of the gradated planes that align in my field. And I find—with the pain of a poet, perhaps, who has sought out his subject and found it in want —I can summon no sorrier pair in creation than the one bearing up at me presently. John Wilkes is still beached in his own slow ruin, mumbling in the sere March grass. V has plucked from somewhere an untimely thistle, which he gums and gives suck to in place of a smoke.

Ain't never turned for tobaccer, he says. Come up from fishing stock myself.

Principle's same either way, I assure him. Out with the old, I tap the harrow's thin blade, and in with the new beneath it.

I weren't never much good with the principles neither. You might want to show me a turn, you got time.

Don't turn yourself in knots, I say. I won't fault you any for an honest mistake.

What other kind is there? he says, on a grin.

He is a finely calibrated sort of a creature, I decide, as I lead him through the gate between yard and field to the terminus of the western row. Here I hitch the harrow in the earth at my feet, which receives the blade as dryly as a pick upon shale.

Though the parry and thrust of our banter is light, suddenly I feel exhausted. Perhaps it's the strain that this wretch and his horse have visited on my idle fancy, or even the season of their coming, which forever ushers with it recollections of the boy, but I find, standing there at the edge of my field with a murder of crows enervating the silence, I can no more expound on the soil's subtleties than account for the presence of him, here, beside me. Without a word to him, I demonstrate turning, pushing the harrow across the stiff ground. He watches from a distance with the thistle in his teeth, sporadically nodding to show that he kens me. The blade of the tool, which has seen better days, pushes no more than a mound out before it.

Futile though it seems, there is something mesmerizing in the scrape of the harrow down the rows. Before long the drifter has fetched up beside me, begins to ape my push-broom motion. All my extremities seize at his nearness. He draws closer still in the beat I have missed. One of his hands clamps over mine, its rough underside bearing down on my knuckles, while the other one fastens on my waist; there, between my ribs and the arch of my hip it explores a whole winter of wallowing in, as if I were a mud-caked sow.

Soon I have ceased to move at all. His nose makes a circuit of my ear.

I'm not—not yet, I say to him, reddening despite myself.

What's that, friend? He draws away. I were just getting the hang of things.

He stands, as if shocked, at his previous distance.

You heard what I said. I unblush. Give it time.

Hell, your call, he says. Well, hell. He picks his teeth. We got all day.

Leaving him there, I head out to my barn to check on the progress of my Burley. The leaves are no more yellow than they were the day before, nor were yesterday than the day before that, but I dote bed to bed on the plants anyway, fingering their spout-sized leaves.

May, I tell the dirt, is a capital month. We will come into our own in May.

The east and west walls of the barn are ventilated to let in light and hasten growth. I keep a different set of shears next to each of the beds to keep them from contagion. Though the impulse to name each bed is there, I fight it away every time it arises.

The line between planter and parent, I think, is one I would rather not cross.

Today, when I have made my rounds, I bide near a wall that peeks out on the field so I can watch my drifter working. It is chillier here than it was outside, and I marshal up the collar of my old brown serge. Though the ventilation slat is about where it should be, I am forced to hang over the seedbed before me to get the eyeful I deserve. Anything less than just that, I decide, would be to part ways with the risk I have taken in allowing this rube and his half-decayed horse the run of my fields and then later my house. He is crude from his hat to the brogues on his feet, with a length of old rope in between for a belt, lest the eyes founder, as mine own have done, in the trench of his laborer's chest. But love is just as crude and common, to speak nothing at all of its shifty-eyed cousin, who is now propelling me through my drawers against the boards in front of me. I take myself out. Experimentally, I pinch. The length of me nods above the dirt, insistent on another one.

Unbidden, the boy appears before me. He is bent across the seedbed that I'm pressed against. I see the tiny freckles in between his shoulder blades. I smell the rooty sweetness, like a brace of cooked carrots, that lives in the space behind his ear. I feel, as his tailbone shifts to receive me, the slow whipstroke of his spine on my stomach. His face is in shadow. I tilt it toward me. But the face is forever retreating from mine. There is only the sameness of our flesh and the musk of the seedbeds beneath us.

Then he's gone and it is still. The memory of him wilts in me. Shaking on the surface of the seedbed below me is the sad ectoplasm he has left me for company, and I bury it quickly, furtively, bitterly, with a deft sweeping motion of my hand.

For the rest of the day—and the day it is long—I keep watch over V from the gills of the barn. He labors inexpertly down the rows, doing work I will have to undo with still more, while the wedge of sky above him hazes over into dusk. The plants are as green as they were when I found them. John Wilkes ripens beneath the big tree. The murder of crows, called home by night, descends once again on the land.

When my stomach gets the best of me, I go check on V where he stands in the field. He has covered a third of it, give or take, which I study with displeasure on my way out to meet him, a long waste of dirt clots and sheered-away roots like the tracks of Poe's Conqueror Worm. He is leaning on the harrow when I reach him, at ease, the same thistle wagging in his teeth.

Tipping his hat, he says, Fine evening. Now wouldn't you say I earned my keep?

Just fine, I lie. You rest a spell. I'll start on supper directly.

Any slops that you have—well I reckon we'll see. John Wilkes is plumb starved to a shade of hisself.

Yes, we'll see, I tell him slowly.

And then, for some reason, I say it again.

While I section out this and then that for a stew I can hear V singing upstairs in the bath. He sings an old Baptist song I know. He sings like a twice-murdered dog, all yelps. The song has a whiff, over the pungency of onions, of the dark, earthy bitters of the Mississippi River where it heaves against the islands of the saved.

As I went down in the river to pray,
Studying about that good old way,
And who shall wear the robe and crown?
Good lord show me the way.
Oh sinners, let's go down, let's go down, come on down.
Oh sinners, let's go down, down in the river to pray.

His voice breaks up around the high notes. A heresy, I muse. Chop, chop. When he reaches the crescendo, I hear a muted thump, as if the Lord God were encircling the drain and V had been called on to save Him.

He ventures downstairs not in the clothes I left for him—a secondhand bunch, but clean, I'd thought—but rather the ones he's been wearing all day and doubtless for many before it. His shoulder-length hair is wet and tangled. His disparate eyes are bright with work. He puts on a show of removing a chair and, hitching his trousers, he eases down in it. As I ladle him stew from behind and above, I see he is rubbing his palms together in a kind of boorish genuflection and scissoring his legs beneath the worn edge of the table.

Lord. Almighty. God, he says, when I am sitting down across. Ain't had a spot of grub like this in I don't know how long.

He chews.

I start: I haven't had a hand...

But then I'm exhausted again. I hush up.

V ravens. I peck. Cicadas buzz. I pour him a cup of mulled wine, which he downs, and taps out his thirst for another.

How long you been out here? he asks, between spoonfuls.

Long enough, I say.

What's that?

I said long enough.

That I gather too long.

To this last thing, I have no answer.

Out on the road for a year most myself. Times is got hard, where I'm from, down in Calvert.

Maryland, then? I say.

That's right. Grandpappy and me—V senior, we'll call him—had a crawdaddy gig on the Chesapeake summers. But hell. With the country like it is, folks is more inclined to step on them than eat them.

Misfortune casts an ample shadow, I say despite myself.

V nods. Pappy lost a leg in Sharpsburg. Hobbles his ass from port to stern. After all that he did for his country... A pause. At least the better half, I reckon. He looks down cockeyed at his soup. Well, *V senior* reckons he's due a sight more than just some Yankee feeb's New Deal.

I say: I suppose.

Can't blame the man much. We got crosses on crosses to bear us, us Rebs.

I try to change the subject. What brings you to Georgia?

It was mainly the next place to be in, I guess. Ask a wandering man why he'd come to a place it doesn't much figure he'd know, do it now?

I don't pretend to know you. Not hardly, I say. I only ask because I'm curious.

Well how long you been queer? he says. Now there's a question begs an answer.

Beg pardon, I say.

You heard me. How long?

I been *queer*, I intone, since I first kissed a girl.

He tilts back in his chair and laughs. The bowls and the cutlery vibrate, then still.

Well I'll be damned, he says. That's fresh. That there's something else.

Your point? I ask.

None such, he says. You tickled me some is the point that I meant.

We focus on the stew in silence—him more than me. I am no longer hungry. He lets his spoon clatter down into the bowl by way of entreating me: seconds. When I come with the pot he has hauled up the wine jug, which he swigs from wholesale, as if it were mash. He eyes me around the rushing neck, his throat spasming with the force of his gulps, and I cannot but wonder, somewhat inopportunely, if his talents at table can be matched in bed.

He lowers the jug and sets it down. I thank you, he says as I refill his bowl.

With wine threading down from the sides of his mouth and his strange eyes clouding with digestion, he puts me in mind of some fiend incubus at the bleary bright end of a tear.

He wipes his mouth and smiles. Goddamn. You sure don't eat much for the chub you got on you.

I figured you needed it more than I did.

You may be right at that, he says. Now what can you do for John Wilkes?

While I clear the table and see to the dishes, V heads outside to attend to his horse. He carries the pail that I use to mop floors, into which I have bailed the stew's remainder, and by the nimbus of gaslight enclosing his passage, he sets it down before John Wilkes. The horse trembles into a standing position and begins to slowly dip its muzzle. V lights a shag cigarette with the lantern and leans against the hitching tree, blowing phantoms of smoke across the yard to the window where I stand, looking out. I can see him and he me, though he better. The tip of his cigarette jewels and dims.

With my forearms submerged in the rusty dishwater, cleaning first a spoon, then a bowl, then a knife, the smooth repetition of my task spins a trance that seems to engender, the harder I stare, from the levitant fire of the cherry.

The boy had left me on a night like this. He had lived with me a week, maybe less. Yes, a week. We had just finished supper and there I was, washing dishes at the sink, when he appeared behind me in the kitchen, in the glass, and announced that he was going for a walk. To take the air, he said, behind, with nothing in him but the air he would take, and I nodded, or did I? Perhaps I said something. Go ahead, or Don't be long, or I'll join you directly. He must've had his satchel, but at the time I did not see it. So I continued to wash, to stare, to expect him. And even when I had finished washing and still the boy had not returned, I thought nothing of it beyond what it was. A jaunt down the road with a cigarette burning while a lover waits inside. And I waited. But the dishes dried, the clock chimed ten, the fire stretched its spine in the grate, and no boy. Eventually, I went outside and spoke his name into the dark. I said it once and said it softly, rigid underneath the stars. And when I said it softly, or because I said it softly, it was then, in that instant of saying, I knew.

I never did yell out to him. I did not even try to follow. And were I to have found him what could I have said, breathless and weakened with pain in the dark, a man gone after a boy half his age down a road filling up, even then, with hot ghosts? He was a student from Atlanta, skipped out mid-term, though I doubt he returned there to take up the pen.

Don Juan I found at the foot of my bed.

This I swept to the floor and sat down in its place.

Tonight, however, he returns. He's standing behind me, slightly warped in the glass, with his hair hanging over his eyes. He is waiting. And I'm ready to notice his satchel this time, the timbre of leaving in his voice, all manner of thing that I failed once to do and have driven myself half to ruin in search of. But when I turn from the sink, now empty of dishes—how terribly empty it is and has been—I find not the boy, but this V, grinning at me.

He pats his lank stomach and stretches his arms. I'm fit to be cooked on a spit, he says. What say that we go on upstairs and get thinner?

After you, I say, and stall, and throttle myself for my weakness. I cough.

He senses this, and eyes me strangely, but turns and begins to ascend anyway.

Unlike myself, he appears in no hurry. Or maybe *hurry*, I consider, is not the right word but that I want this to be done with, somehow, without doing. His backside shifts before my face. I smell his smoke, his sweat, his dinner. At the landing the drifter makes straight for my room with an uncanny sense for the door that conceals it, and the moment—no more—leaves me deathly afraid that he's been *in* the room between bath-time and supper, or else has been dogging my prospects for weeks, making note of my hours, predilections and habits, bivouacked in the dark of the liminal fields as I move through the half-lighted rooms in my robe. He goes through the door and he leaves it drawn open. I peer behind me down the stairs, through a veil of liquid shadow, to the foyer. I follow in dread of not only what waits—V nude, V clothed, V swaddled in furs, V's body with Benjamin's face or vice-versa—but also of whether that half-part of me that is still hesitating in the dark of the landing will be able to cleave, when the business is done, to the half that has gone on ahead. But they've already tussled, the latter won out. I am inside the room, at the foot of the bed. Curiously, V has shucked one shoe and one trouser leg, but is otherwise clothed. He is contending with the half that remains when I enter, sitting there on the bed with his feet on the floor. Such a weird and impractical mode of undressing, I note to myself, standing speechless in front of him.

In the event of a fire, or some other calamity—which seems rather likely under present circumstances—he would have to go fumbling down the stairs, one-shoed and half-trousered, to save his skin.

Come on and get comfortable, friend. He pats the bed. Remake yourself like the Good Lord intended.

I kick off my shoes and my socks, drop my trousers and lever my shirt above my head but resolve to abide in my drawers for the moment, which to my dismay have decided to tent. I am twice dismayed to realize that I have undressed in advance of my guest, who although trouser-less still wears his shirt in observance of some rule of the house—my house—that I've failed to heed altogether. He leans half-clothed against the headboard, flipping through the very book, which I must've neglected to hide before supper. In a brisk, awkward shuffle, with my fingers picking air, I come around to where he sits.

Please, I tell him. Put it back. A costly book you're holding there.

Is it now? he says, delighted. And to think I been wasting my time with crawdaddy's.

First edition of its kind. Please, I say. No disrespect…

He eyes me levelly for a time with Don Juan spread in his hands. Then shuts it.

Exhausted again, I sit on the bed. My eyes dart from V's bottom half to the book, which is safe, at least for now, in its place on the side-table.

Enough with books. A lengthy pause. Unless you was planning on reading it to me.

It dawns on me that he is right. Desire, like a freak of hot wind, blows me to him, and before I can fully apprehend the feel of his lips beneath my own I am kissing his mouth, kissing through it and past it, toward a mouth that's unreachable, hidden within. V gives a grunt of surprise. The mouth moves. I grope up his leg, and find him flaccid. But then, as I kiss, something starts to grow there. Finally I get a purchase. His body heaves beneath my own, trying to buck me off or over, so I pinion him there with the force of my lips but cannot hold for long. He flips me. I can feel myself falling, first up, then down, until I'm at staring height with the paisleys that leer from the stitch of the covers.

I can see that you're given to leading, says V, holding me still above the bed. We got a different way of waltzing where I'm from, friend. Let's see if you can keep up.

He levers my drawers to my feet, slaps my backside. I feel his handprint blooming there.

I'm not ready yet, I say in a whisper, but the pressure is mounting against my spine.

With a few ragged thrusts, he is finished. He shudders. Already I feel him growing softer; he slips, by degrees, from inside me.

How long has it been, tenderloin? he says hoarsely.

Clearing his throat, he withdraws and dismounts. He fly swats my backside by way of farewell.

I hear him padding round the bed until he appears on the opposite side. At a glance I can see that the locus between us has shifted irretrievably into his camp. His eyes are fixed on me with chilly appraisal, as if I were an apple within thieving distance whose ripeness he is measuring.

Hunkered there, I cannot move. I feel only dampness, the torque of my muscles. In my ears is a rushing that ebbs and flows according to the angle of my head above the covers.

I might take a bath, I tell him then.

Why tenderloin, I'm hurt, he says. And all of this time I had thought we was peas.

I rise wordlessly and head off to bathroom. Before I shut the door, out of the corner of my eye, I see V reaching for the book on the side-table, but the effort it takes to warn him off is not within my power.

So I don't.

In the bathroom I run the taps to hot and consider the man who stands there in the mirror. He has a limp and impoverished head of hair, like the leavings of some jungle spider. His eyes are impacted in his face, and banked with charcoal-colored circles. His lips are full, but also thin, perhaps on account of the frown that he wears, and his sudden, sharp chin, with its bit of grey stubble, sets off the wattles of his neck. Below he is stocky in curious places—in the chest, at the hips and high up on the arms. His drawers are bunched around his ankles, like a puddle he is standing in.

I look at this man and blink him gone, but when I open my eyes he is still there before me. So I turn altogether from the mirror, toward the tub, which appears, in the steam, to be filling itself. Before getting in, I give the man a parting glance. The backs of his thighs are trickling blood. The bathwater pinkens with blood when he's in it and I look for the man, but he's nowhere. He's gone. The water ascends to the lip and then over. I watch it melt across the tiles. The tap is still roaring around my bulk, so I twist the water off and sit. I have been sitting for a minute, or maybe an hour, when I hear a faint knock on the door of the bathroom. Like a mesmerist's bell, it brings me back and I sit up more still and more straight in the tub.

Tenderloin, I hear.

The knock.

Oh, tenderloin.

A chill runs through me.

I try to stand but sit back down still clutching, both-handed, the rim of the tub.

Tenderloin. Now don't be shy. I just want to parlay with you.

Just a minute, I say, with concern in my voice, as if the man at the door is a guest I'm neglecting.

Open up, says the voice. It's dull out here. Ain't nothing but me and a old empty bed.

Just a minute, I repeat, and find my arms and legs are shaking.

The water, hard water, so slightly discolored, is dullest gray shot through with pink. It makes me think of many things. It makes me think of sundown, winter.

The voice at the door clears its throat and is silent. I know I cannot face its owner. But neither remain in the place where I am with that voice and the throat that compels it abroad, crooning their filth throughout my house with an eye for my rarer editions, my silver.

But after all, what *is* our pre-sent state? the voice begins behind the door. Tis' bad and may be better, all men's lot. Most men are slaves, no more so than the great, to their own…wu-hims and pashuns…and what not. So-city itself, which should create kineness, destroys what little we had got. To feel for none is the true…is the true…soshul art of the world's…sto…stoics…men without a heart.

Though shorn of their music, I cotton the words. I must've read the passage, thought it lovely, underlined it; I struggle to recall the stanza. They are likely from Canto V, I think, given the mention of *slaves and society*, and uttered by him *of English look* to whom our hero, Don Juan, has been chained on the galley.

The situation has escaped me. I cannot say what I will do.

Just now a black old…nutrel…person-age…, the voice continues, reading on.

But I cannot brook another word and call out, Come in. The door's open. Come in.

The door swings in and there stands V. He is bare as the day, with the book in his hands. The hair he wears upon his chest and down the funnel, headed south, is patterned not unlike the grass that has come up these past couple weeks in the thaw—isolate patches of brown, here and there, with skin swirled in among them. His genitals hang between his legs like the innards of an unswung bell.

What took you so long, tenderloin? I's about to give up hope. Now where was I? he says, drawing closer, adjusting a pair of phantom glasses, pointing to the center of the gorgeous, foolish book with a brutal stabbing motion in the crease of it, the heart.

I'm suddenly wrathful: Put it down.

Who are you to say who can read and who can't?

It's my book, I tell him. And you're not one.

Is that how it is? He ruffles the pages. It is *your* house, at that, he says. Though I don't reckon you pulled rank when I had you bent over the bed a sight back.

Give it here, I tell V, sitting up in the bath.

What's that, tenderloin? He readjusts the phantom glasses.

I stand up dripping and lunge for the book, but he capers around me out of reach.

Don't be a fool, I say. My foot slips. So I grab at the shower rod to steady myself.

Peering over the…capt-ives…he seemed to mark their look and age…he continues to read from the book while evading.

I bring a leg over the lip of the tub, still holding onto the shower rod. He slips a little, too, as he maneuvers with the book, but steadies himself on the thick window mold that juts above the bathtub's foot and having done so pushes off, which brings him back within my reach. Getting hold of the book, I yank back. He resists. A page tears away in my hand. I cry out.

Goddamn you, I tell him. Stop your clowning.

He looks at me with something approaching recognition, but it just as soon thins in the width of his grin. In the pause that ensues, I lunge again, reaching not for the book but for his arm and with a sudden and bewildering access of strength, I start to pull him toward the bath. Abandoning horseplay, he tries to resist me, but I have got the upper hand. We saw back and forth, interlocked, across the water, while the shower rod rattles above us. The tiles are wet, the bath is full; we skid toward the water, then back, then toward. Ours is a comical struggle, I think, in yet another moment of panicked omniscience. The shower rod starts to unmoor from the wall in a thin dusting of plaster.

When the rod finally gives, it is me that goes yelping, as if I were about to fall, but when the echo of it fades I find that I am still upright. V lies humped across the bath. His head must've knocked going down, for it bleeds. The water where I stand, which has near absorbed my own blood, is rapidly blushing again with my guest's. For a time, watching him, I cannot think. His feet stir a bit on the tile. He moans. At first it relieves me to see him returning, but then

I look down and catch sight of the book. It lies submerged beneath the water, bits of pulp that were its pages drifting up to the surface.

I lift him up beneath the arms. I haul him in the brimming tub. Then I hold his face against the bottom, near the drain, where a chaos of bubbles starts to fume. But with each go at breathing he swallows more water until his legs and back are seizing. He is trying to move his limbs, I realize, trying to buck me, to make me submit, but the weight of the water invading his lungs and depriving his brain of the air that it needs has rendered his movement pathetic and slurred, like a swamp-trammeled horse with a case of distemper. He surges for the nearby drain, attempting to pull it with his teeth. For a moment I fear he will succeed and I move to restrain him with still greater violence, grinding his nose against the tub while he snaps at the pull-chain, his hair in his face, this new path of action availing him little apart from the water that now floods his mouth, his strivings becoming subaqueous screams that the water might only unleash if it could. A huge gout of water erupts to the surface, heaves against my clutching hands.

When he's finished I rise and watch him, still. The waters about his head are peaceful. A tiny wave fleeing the things that it's seen unrolls to the foot of the tub, and breaks there.

I'm secure in my skin as I've not been in months. I am perfectly aware of the measures I take. The shower curtain tears from the rod with a shriek. I lay it out across the tiles. V is lead-heavy in death, a behemoth. I lever him over the lip of the tub and onto the curtained tile. He smacks. Rolling him in is a tricky maneuver given the narrowness of the bathroom, but by and by I manage, manipulating his limbs, until, at the door, I have him wound. I open the door, and step over his body. Once in the hall, I drag him out. The stairs are a whole other matter completely. With an eye for efficiency, I shuttle him down. His trip to the bottom is anxious and fitful. For a moment I fear he will catch on the banister. But my fears are allayed by a final corkscrew that tumbles him into the foyer.

I go out to the shed and take down an undertaker, the shotgun I use for rare bird-sits. I move through the darkness between shed and house, the undertaker's hardware creaking. I am hunting up John Wilkes, still roped to the tree in the yard where V left him. When I come round the side of the house, he is standing. He spooks under weight of the buckles and winches.

There, I tell him. Easy now.

One huge, liquid eye regards me.

I tether V fast just in front of the pommel. The horse snorts and stamps, but I soothe him, V-style. With the shotgun riding in my boot and V's shrouded body seesawing out before me, I get the horse's engine running with a couple anonymous kicks to its ribs. The birches drift past me like stygian sentries with the moon moving hungrily in between, and the night into which I foray with my payload is as fey and unreal as a vaudeville curtain. Mile by mile, the birches dwindle. The land begins to open out. I turn due east down a little-traveled road, and John Wilkes high-steps through the brush. Night birds call from out the dark, the bramble yields beneath my mount and V's murdered body whispers murder in its tether like a voice telling me to turn back. But I don't. Before long Powmahatta Lake glitters through gaps in the trees north of me, and I hector John Wilkes straight ahead, to its bank. I tie the horse fast, then contend with the body. It slips through my hands with residual bathwater. I cradle it down from the loosened undertaker, and lay it in the mud.

As I drag the body lakeward by a corner of the curtain, my socks ride low about my ankles. The moon is unnaturally bright overhead, and through the membrane of the curtain I can just make out V's face. By and by, I reach the bank. I orient the mass and push. The body takes to water and glides from the bank. For a moment I fear, as I did on the stairs and before that the killing tub, that my calculations will not serve, but the body compasses in an arc across the lake, dips its prow and starts to sink. When its legs are slant above the surface, I find I can no longer look. And as the rest goes under, gurgling, a stale rooty scent reaches me on the shore.

I rise with the shotgun and climb the wet bank to where the dead man's horse is reined. He warns me off with twitching ears, an anxious four-step where he stands, but I come on while breaching the shotgun for business. I press it just beneath his ear. An eruption of bone-meal and moon-blackened blood leaps over the trail and makes rain in the brush. He wavers above the dirt, then sits. The shot resounds across the lake. I lever the shell, untie the undertaker and make my way home through the dark.

*   *   *

Spring storms come. I watch the road. Dust rises and wafts between the rains, climbing my clapboard fence, my trellises, until faintly it tickles my nose, and I sneeze. There are figures on the road again, more with every passing day. And these pilgrims are weirder still than those who came a month before, as though the spring carries some sinister spoor, some airborne kudzu on it, drifting. Man-children in cheap black suits; wretched and toothless Methuselahs, shuffling; ethereal girls touting baskets of laundry who embroider the birdsong with low, meek laments. Where can they be headed, now? Perhaps there is a carnival detraining in Eatonton. Or perhaps they are headed nowhere in particular, a place I am already in, without walking.

I have ceased to see the boy at all. It is the first spring in three years that he hasn't come calling. I see figures like him, sure enough, with the same slight build and dreamy gait, but they become what they are within a few yards of the window, and I lean back in my chair, benumbed. Even in the curing barn, where the ghost of our congress haunts the beds, I am alone with my plants as I have not been in years. Enterprising breezes affirm through the slats. It is the plants alone that stand to gain from quiet fecundity of the season, and they yellow at rates that supersede my ability or willingness to

21

trim them up healthy. Sowing days are fast approaching. I turn and re-turn the waiting soil. Mornings the wind-brought fog is thicker, and I do not venture out until well after noon, afraid that I will lose my way like a child in a fairy tale labyrinth.

My reading habits have devolved. I now read exclusively novels, no verse; and not by the authors that trammel the mind when one talks of 'novels' with a capital N, but rather the maudlin fever-dreams of Stoker, Lewis and Walpole, whose carnivorous worms, libertine monks and castles filled with vengeful spirits allow me to drift outside myself where the past is only that. I tried for a while to take in The Prelude to supplement the book I'd lost, but the nostalgia of the poem depressed me, and I made it no more than a quarter way through. As I read in my parlor, by candlelight now, for the nights are lukewarm and dismissive of fires, I sometimes lace my chamomile with a bit of long-neglected Scotch. Yet I always add a dash of cinnamon and clove to keep the moment festive. As for the book I can no longer read, I have fashioned it a shroud out of silk handkerchiefs. It lies in a shoebox in my closet, consoled by the whisper of coats, I imagine, whenever I come to retrieve one. I no longer bathe in the washroom upstairs and seldom use its sink or toilet. I have constructed a bathing shed out back to which I siphon heated water. And though I flirt with whooping cough in the twenty-yard dash between bath-shed and house, the discomfort of this is a small price to pay when I think on its alternative.

Mid-month I go to lay my crop and find an unpleasant surprise waiting for me. In the field's northwest corner, beneath the shadow of the water tower, a bulge is forming in the soil. It is not visible, or not yet anyway, to the probings of the naked eye, but responds to the weight of my steps thereupon it; it is not quite a softness but neither a hardness—a viscous plumpness in the earth. I set my seedbed on the ground and trace its limits with my toe. It has a circumference of five feet or so. Its seam describes a sloppy oval. I stand at its center and adjust my spring weight, leaning foot to foot in an exploratory two-step. An outgoing ripple traverses the mound and dies where the dirt flattens out at its edges. I wonder if it can be popped with the harrow, but decide not to risk it when I picture its contents flooding the otherwise healthy rows. So perhaps when I venture out tomorrow, the bulge will have magically drained itself. The earth has witching in her ways. I have never pretended to know her completely. So I pick up my seedbed, head back to the barn and occupy the rest of my day with trimming.

But when I come the next day, the bulge has increased—a quarter in size, give or take, overnight. I see it now a yard away by the depth of the shadow it casts in full sun, the soil on its surface a shade or two darker than the biscuit-colored flats around it. I walk to the center this time, and bounce. My stomach responds with a lurch to the ripple, which glugs audibly to the edges this time. And it might be the sun or the turn things have taken or the pint of Scotch I drank last night, but I am suddenly as dizzy as a sparrow in a gale and find I must sit down. There's nowhere to sit but where I stand. The guts of the bulge redistribute beneath me. Sitting cross-legged with my chin in my hand a foot or so above the field I watch the crows strafing the furrows for worms with sharp, incoming cries. I sit there, say, an hour or more. And I've carried, while sitting, to calm, clockless regions where there's only the sky, and the field, and these birds. But then I return and animate; my field does the same, breaking free of its tableau. Standing up tensed for the shudder beneath me, I make my way back to the house.

The next day I go out to Penderton's place to pick his mind about the bulge. He is a thin, grizzled man with red-rimmed eyes and the handshake of a public statue; I have wondered at times if Stonewall Jackson, commanding the traffic on Eatonton Square, isn't somehow a descendant of his, whatever his bellum allegiances. He's especially stony today as we walk, irritated, perhaps, by what he perceives to be hasty incompetence on my part in tending to my own five acres. He walks a beeline down the road, his gaze dragging sullenly past the birches, responding to my cluck with, Well..., or Yep, or Reckon that's the case. But when we arrive in my field he stops short and appraises the bulge with a hand in his whiskers. I wait in the water tower's shade while he circles it up close. Even from several yards away, I can see it has doubled in size overnight; it retards my neighbor's pokes and prods with a volley of liquid shrugs.

Penderton comes to stand beside me.

What do you think it could be? I ask.

Irrigation block? he posits.

I've checked for that, I tell him.

And I have—good and well. All the ducts were unobstructed.

Well, he says, and rubs his chin. His eyes go thin, as if to will an explanation.

What? I say, and turn to face him. Whatever it is you can tell me. I'll weather.

Soil's loose enough, rainwater jams up. Call it hard water because it's hard-headed. Refuses to mosey along, like a squatter.

But can't it be drained? I say, with a quaver. Can't it be flushed, or ironed out?

He shakes his head. Nothing for it but to wait. So late in spring—he sucks his gums—your tract won't brook that kind of meddling.

But I'm due to start planting this week, I say. I don't have that kind of time.

Patience is as patience does. Looks like you'll have to make time, he says.

I stare at him in disbelief and slowly shake my head. You're the expert.

I don't pretend to be, he says. I just tend to tell the truth.

I wait as Penderton advised, but the bulge continues to grow exponentially. I begin to suspect it was eavesdropping on us, and hastens its growth as a tactical measure. Its circumference was just five feet at first, then eight the next day, then fourteen on the following, and has stretched to nearly one-hundred-and-thirty by the end of the factory week. Despite having roots in my field's northwest corner—if whatever gives it succor can be called *roots*—it refuses to follow northwesterly ways, but pours itself, instead, due south. This might be due largely, or so I concede, to the thing's oval shape, since tapered to a teardrop; it has the silent momentum of candlewax as it creeps through the strata of my field. But this is not to say I'll let it. I have already taken a studied defensive. I scribble its measurements in a daybook, not just its circumference, but also its height, which reaches my ankle at its highest, only to leaven a bit, further south. I liken it to household goods, or whatever resemblance I have, then, to mind—molasses at first, then a gelatin mold, in the following days, hardened grease, salt taffy, the putty I use as a stopgap for leaks. It is hardest in the driving phallic shadow of the tower, and softens the closer you get to its hem; it could be compared to a sunny-side egg were it only half as round as one, yet it squares with no symmetry known or imagined apart from the constancy of its growth, spilling down across my rows like pork-fat on a griddle.

But all my comparisons seem inadequate. What have I, really, to liken it to?

It is congealing from the inside out, or maybe the outside in—I am uncertain. Charting its growth, my attitude shifts between clinical interest and loathe fascination, borne on the same undercurrent of fear. I have felt, on my hikes from end to end, stopping betimes to notate in my book, not unlike some manner of naturalist poet on the verge of a new topographic discovery; but then, as my data accumulates and its dread implications disorder the page, I come back to myself and freeze mid-step. All the exultance drains out of me.

One day as I stand at the edge of the bulge, drawing my daily diagram, I see that the crows have restricted their hunt to the healthy land beyond its borders. Every so often one veers down toward it, tensing its feet to make good on a worm, but the others recant it just short of its meal in a riot of brotherly squawks.

It is on this day I start to sense a sort of pall above my field.

For a while I'd ascribed it to nothing so much as the dread that the bulge provoked in me—a dread which, I reasoned, any man would've felt on finding himself the caretaker of land cultivating itself against his wishes—but today, as I watch the crows divert and find myself more muddle-headed by the minute, I suspect that my dread is more than dread, at least in the standardest sense of the word; even *palpable dread* is too polished and pat to get at what I'm driving toward. It is a physical phenomenon that cloaks itself as an aberration of the mind, so near to imperceptible that any who sense it must question themselves as to how they do. It is a pale emanation, without sound or smell, but no less immediate for its blandness. It covers the bulge from end to end, is strongest in the northwest corner and tickles my sense like the film of a bubble, or a veil of scentless gas. This bad air compounds my panic, for how am I to drain the air? And if it can repair itself, as Penderton seems to have faith my field will, then how should I venture to judge a renewal of the medium through which I move?

Nights my dysphoria steadily worsens. I do not read a word or try. I've abandoned the pretense of lacing my tea with a couple restorative splashes of Scotch but instead fill my mug to brimming over with the stuff and swallow it down like a honky-tonk brawler.

I should really invest in a couple of tumblers to civilize my excess.

I do not drink, per say, to dream, but to rout the bad air from invading my house. The liquor kills my keenness to it, lulls me in a pleasing way, whereas the bad air, with its own lulling properties, does this most unpleasantly. And so drunken and joyless on Scotch and bad air—for in spite of my efforts the bad air abides—I wander the rooms of my house without object, picking up items at random, strange items, items I no longer recognize, and having made a study of each curio while turning it over in my hands, I put it down in a place it was not meant to go, only to find it again in the morning, a refugee of meaning or purpose.

Sometimes I end up in parts of the house that I have no business being in or look down to find something clutched in my hands that I would prefer not to see there. I once found myself in the washroom upstairs, peering into the vacancy of the tub, as if the bare rod had begotten a curtain that I was attempting to see through. Once I came to in the dark of the pantry with Byron's poem in my hands, trying to decipher in all earnestness the warped hieroglyphs on the page.

I promptly dropped it.

And then, on a Sunday, surveying my field while tallying my speculations, I see someone come round the side of my house with a bedroll yoked across its back. I shut my daybook and I go out to meet it at a pace that concerns me as cagily brisk, so I slow walking over the hem of the bulge, which has by now reached the field's midpoint. Seeing me approach, the figure slows, too. It stops at the edge of the field, behind the fence. Drawing closer, I see through the old wattle-boards that there is something familiar in its stance; a studiously lazy slouch with one arm crooked upon its waist, the other one massaging the back of its neck. It is a boy of fifteen years or so who bears an uneasy resemblance to a man I once knew. He has shoulder-length hair and a sinewy build and his clothes tell the story of his travels, and his poverty. Up close I can see that his eyes, though aligned, have the same pale blue cologne all through them.

Fine afternoon, says the boy.

His voice echoes.

Startled, I stop short. Hi there.

Don't mean to put you out, he says, eyeing the daybook beneath my arm. But if you'll oblige me a spell, I'd be mighty.

I'm just in the middle of something, I say.

He nods and he grins. It won't take but a minute. Come down around these parts from Calvert.

I watch him for a moment through the slats of the fence. He's a snake not got its bite, a gardener.

Well, I feed him slowly, breathing. What can I do for you, son?

I thank you, he says. Much obliged to you, sir. I'm hunting my big brother Virgil? Virgil Stokes? He come round this way too, in winter. He were looking for work and what goes. Might you seen him?

After a pause, I say, What's he look like?

Well, says the boy, with another shy grin. He looks a lot like me, I guess. We're brothers through and through, us Stokes, though I guess he'd have told you his name were just V.

You're the one person like you I've seen.

The boy's eyes thin; they study mine.

You sure you ain't seen him? He were coming this way. Likely as not, he'd have ridden right past you. Got an old straw horse he calls John Wilkes. Your neighbor to the south—Penderton is his name—turned V away hisself he says.

I keep to myself out here, I say. Widower, I volunteer. Country like it is, I say, who can you trust these days but that?

Amen. The boy chuckles. Now there's the truth of it. But my brother Virgil, he's one you can trust. We's reared to be trusted, us Stokes. He nods gravely. But I guess you ain't seen him and that is all right.

I'm afraid that I haven't, I say. I've been busy. I permit myself a genuine smile.

Grandpappy, he says. He passed in March. I reckon that Virgil ought to know.

Well, I'm sorry to hear that, I tell him. I am.

Pnuemonier took him, rest his soul.

He giveth and taketh and giveth, I say.

I wince at the sound of my words, but they fit.

The boy adjusts his bedroll, puts a hand through the fence. I take it in mine, shake it weakly and drop it. And it might be the suddenness of my greeting or something the boy has been turning in mind, but I've only just let go his hand when he freezes and looks out on the field behind me.

Pleased to meet you, he says, a bit stiff, half-distracted.

Likewise, I say.

We are shooting the breeze.

But then he says: Field's got a funny pitch to it. Won't do well to plant in that.

I cannot slow my heartbeat down. My eyes raise a little, then drop to my feet.

Thing is, he begins, I'm in fishes myself, but I just might could help you some.

I bought the land cheap, I say. Years ago. On account of the pitch, as you say. But I've managed.

You sure about that? he says, staring harder. Cause it's some folks manage better with a second set of eyes. If you got a plow and some horses, a level, I could help you shave that pitch right out. Or on second thought, Mister—

No thank you, I say. I've earned my keep here five years running.

What you got going out there? Some tobaccer?

But I've already turned from the fence with a nod, and what he says next is inaudible. And so I keep walking without looking back, but I can sense him there, behind me. I walk on the skirt of the bulge, then its nexus, beginning to feel as I walk like Lot's wife, and the quiver beneath my flexing feet is a welcome distraction from turning around when all of a sudden I'm nigh a mile distant and practically stepping on Penderton's spores and now close enough to my neighbor's outbuildings that I swear I can make out the eyes of his Negroes observing me, too, from behind the smeared windows, the squinted blue eyes and the big staring brown ones drawing, between them, a cross-hairs on me. Then I stop and turn around. The figure of Young Stokes is gone. There is only the pitch of my malformed field, and the coffinmaker's angles of my house.

When I am done taking stock of the bulge for the day, I return to the house and do not leave. My hands have been shaking something awful, a tremor that dies, to my dismay, when I have had a drink. And when I've had another, more stiff than the first, my mind begins to circle the encounter with Stokes, pouncing on fears that I've had all long, but refused until now to acknowledge. So I take to the stairs, mounting two at time, until I am in the bathroom. There, I turn the tub up hot and I shake out a thick coat of lye in its basin. I scour the porcelain overlong. A clay-colored stratum begins to bleed through. And when I relent, the rag tight on my knuckles—a readymade bandage if they, too, are bleeding—the tub is less clean than it was at the outset and porcelain shavings clog the drain. Ignoring the damage, I hunt up a mop, and I do to the floor as I did to the tub. The tile does not flake as the porcelain did, but the mop snaps in two midway through the job. I toss away the splintered halves. I stand at the sink, staring into the mirror. The whites of my eyes are infested with red. I stare until bad air clouds the glass. Then I go into the bedroom.

There I strip the paisley covers, carry them down to the unheated parlor. I lay a bed of kindling in the cold fireplace, bundle the covers and chase with a match. The goose-feather takes with a vacuous whoosh. The flames burns high and hale; they raven. Renegade feathers escape the fire, some of them charred and some still burning, so I unfold the gate from the compromised hearth and stomp them into smudges. But feathers continue to blow from the flames on an updraft of smoke curling into the parlor. The bad air fills with small red sparks that I swat like a bear in an immolate forest. The flue must be jammed, or roaring with backdraft, for my eyes start to sting and the room grows vague. I run to the kitchen and fill up a bucket, which I see, running back, has a rime of old stew; I cripple the flames with a great, slow splash, which releases a sour charnel smell and more smoke. I drop the bucket, fan the air. Through a topcoat of ash, my knuckles bleed. I am filthy from head to toe. Night has fallen.

I decide to take a leap of faith. I must kill the bulge where it lives, now or never.

So I put on my coat and head out to the shed, where I lift down a pick from the hooks. Approaching the field, the bad air coalesces, so I slog through the darkness while oaring my arms. I can see the summit of the bulge. It rears from the mist now coating the field like Leviathan's hump, or a dune on a beach. I climb, up and up. The mist chases thin. I crest at the top and I bounce, the pick swinging. The vitals beneath me retreat, a raw nerve. I fall a couple steps sideways.

As I steady the pick above my head, preparing to spike the thing's nerve-center, I cannot but think on what grim melodrama, what sad penny dreadful I've wandered into, and then, for the first time in ages, I laugh. I laugh and I spike it. The pick follows through. My arms follow through. Or the pick. They are one. A geyser of something leaps into the air. And the part of the bulge where I'm standing deflates with a curious-smelling exhalation—a secret humid, fungal smell, like a flooded root cellar, or a log's underside, or the water in my middle ear after a long summer swim in Powmahatta. It is what the bad air has been gesturing at, the character it's been circling.

A slow upwelling of indistinct fluid begins to wash around the pick. It bubbles first, then trickles, flows, in a current that breaks around my feet and reforms down the slope behind me. When I wrench the pick toward me the topsoil gives way with the light ripping sound of old canvas. More fluid wells down the length of the cut, and something gelatinous winks at me between its shredded ridges.

So I make my way back to my first entry-point, reinsert the pick and drag. I scalpel the bulge across its summit; fluid cascades all which ways. I set the pick down. I no longer need it. The ground has become, of a sudden, consenting. Both-handed, I take up a loose flap of topsoil and flay it neatly from the seam. This I repeat with the opposite flap. Soon a sub-bulge, slick, translucent, has been laid bare beneath the first. But unlike the earthworks that formerly hid it, the sub-bulge resists my excavations. Trying to gouge my fingers in it is like trying to stir a pot of clay. The pick is again necessary, and I fetch it, and sink it down into that jelly. There is no upwelling this time as before—just a quiver, a sigh and the night, up above me.

The sub-bulge disinters in chunks: triangular, square, globular, trapezoidal. They shake in the sling of the pick as I lift them, and they shimmer in the watchful moon, and they glom, awkwardly, to the base of the bulge where they give up their jelly, becoming as stone. And the mass, as I hack it, is stiffening, too, due to some alchemy of the air, and each good swing demands one better, which I give and I give, until I am panting. By grades the stuff reveals its veins, an armature of bone-like roots. I dig and heave, I hack and tear, and the pick sees me on with a crackling force, and I think of the copse at the edge of my field that I will have to clear this summer, a snarl of parched and fire-prone limbs that will fall to the flat of my axe, moving outward, and yet for the present I'm not moving outward, I remind myself, no, I am traveling down, and the resonance of it, but also the strangeness, renders my progress vertiginous, endless.

The armature elaborates the further down I trim it back, while the layer of gelatin is thinning. I clear the bramble, wrenching, stabbing, plunging the pick with my foot, like a shovel, and the weave of it shatters, caving in, emitting a sort of particulate dust like bad air given solid form, and I sneeze violently, several times. I sneeze blood.

And suddenly I'm at the core.

The armature takes on a definite shape.

It is similar in concept to the ribs of a man, but instead of inverting and forming a hollow, describes a perfect, slatted orb. The orb hangs suspended, some ten feet deep, on a chandelier structure that draws its support from the earthen walls around it. It recalls, to my thinking, a trinket of bone hung from a well's pulley system. Gently, I insert the pick between the interstices of the orb and pry. These inmost parts give way less readily, as if clinging fast to whatever they harbor, but by and by I wrench them free.

The onion has been skinned.

A globular sac which, at first glance, is two times the size of a healthy watermelon, depends from the top of the slatted orb by a thin albino membrane. It sways in a faint subterranean breeze. The membrane continues around the sac and through it I see, like cracks in a relic, a tracery of veins.

32

I look to the top of the hole I've dug, through a labyrinth of roots and clinging dirt, and just as I do, the moon passes over, and dyes the darkness brighter.

The membrane wrapped around the sac has a sturdier weave than I'd initially thought. But I manage to tear a dime-sized hole, and step back to see what will happen. The hole in the membrane widens further, the membrane retracts around the sac and an exhalation of bad air leaks into the darkness. But nothing save air is released in that darkness. Nothing goes scuttling off, newly born. Contrary to all my expectations, its insides are a total void. The sac has collapsed upon itself and it sways raggedly in the tunneling breezes. I scrub at my face, find my nose is still bleeding.

I let the pick drop and it finds something soft.

I study the ground, or what passes for ground in these bleak reaches of the earth, and discover not mud, as I'd thought, but a bulge, gestating in darkness beneath the bulge prior. But this one is balder, and softer, and smaller, a polyp striving towards the skin. It's a sub-sub-bulge, afterbirth of its brother. It even bears the faintest sheen. I fetch up the pick. It feels heavy, gummed up. I heft it and hold it aloft, undecided.

There is nothing left to do but dig. There is nowhere left to go but down. And so dig down I do, with a mournful intensity. Gelatinous layers, bone-like roots, the chandelier structure, the slatted orb and there, at its core, the same pale sac, the same decoy of life inside it. Carefully, I part the membrane. As with the first, it retracts and hangs open. And though I am certain that I will find nothing before I sink the pick again, something keeps me digging, something hopeful and alarmed, something that insists that so much digging is bound to yield up some reward.

The water-logged body of my boarder. The headless remnants of his horse. An unborn version of the boy, coiled on himself with his thumb in his mouth and his beautiful eyes shut tight. One of many boys, so many, that I have known across the years: dustbowl boys in dusty hats; soldier boys on R & R; stable boys from three towns over who whinnied and strove as I broke them in bed; a mountebank's boy who would wear, in my presence, one white, erotic, calfskin glove, and practiced with it, up my spine, the very magic he was versed in.

I revisit these moments, ten times, then again, but the living of them has already been done. Yet in hope or despair, I return to them always, determined to live them correctly this time, only to find, in the maze of my efforts, that I am back where I began.

The opportunity of them has fallen to ashes. The scent I'm chasing has gone cold.

A succession of caves unfolds before me, honeycombed beneath the earth, and I wonder, vaguely, how it is that the system bears up before such excavation. Surely, some crawlspace, some chamber to come, will crumble in to bury me. And I see myself now, burrowing through the strata, mute and intense, like an ant in a farm, consoled by the knowledge that where I am headed is where, at last, I'll want to be.

The world opens up like a bud—this I know. And seem to grasp its inner workings. Though as for my own, they remain hidden from me, as they have always been.

The Man Who Noticed Everything

Clemens came into the town of Ulrich on a black stretch of road that went among cedars. Fall was giving up the ghost. A heavy ground-fog searching low on the asphalt so that Clemens appeared to begin at the ankles; the magic-lantern shapes of trees, slimming Route 80 to a vanishing point; the character of the air itself, a mixture of wood-smoke, industrial fumes and the humors of the shedding pines. Clemens noticed everything. All he had with him was a foam bedroll, a backpack stuffed with puzzles and a trinket full of lavender; this last item he wore on a necklace to keep his senses keen while walking and the sound of the sediment washing around the inside of the metal ball pricked along his vertebrae every time he heard it. Alone of his kind, the stranger called Clemens, walking down other peoples' roads.

Clemens decided to break with the road to try his luck at finding some shelter. He was tired. The upper portion of his back was clad in a snakeskin of third-degree burns that made it hard for him to walk for unbroken miles at a time, as he wanted. Clemens did not know what the burns symbolized, nor when he had received them, nor why in that region. Only that they were mild for third-degree burns, but had not been given time enough to heal, even so. To wit he had broken a couple of ribs, most likely around the same time he'd been burned, and the ruin of them on these cold nights of walking was intangibly worse than the burns on his skin. For Clemens had the notion he was not a vain man. He needed only at the moment to be functional.

The lights fell away, the trees, then Clemens. He could not see his swinging hands, the toes of his journey-worn sneakers. No moon. Out past the treeline the land tended upwards through a field of tall grass, stiff already with a light rigor mortis of frost. Clemens stopped walking at the top of the rise to stretch the pain out of his ribs and to air the raw skin underneath his wool flannel, something he did not because of the pain, but because he was the kind of man who did not stop without good reason. Then he saw lights a half-mile distant, straining myopically out of the fog, which had risen to the height of his waist since the road, and seemed to rise yet at an even steeper gradient the further out you got into the field, toward the lights. Which came from a house, Clemens slowly observed. Rambling, farm-style, long and low. So Clemens stood in more than just a field; this was property. But Clemens had not seen the signs.

The unmarked holding where he stood was bordered to the east by a line of dark trees, and these formed a T with the long stand of cedars that bordered Route 80 into Ulrich. He made for the farmost stand of trees, which slowly revealed themselves as poplars, and beneath their autumn scantness he prepared to pitch his bed. But Clemens drew up short when he saw there in front of him a row of irregular shapes in the dark that extended along the line of trees northerly into the property. Graves. A thin isthmus of them, twenty yards long, headstone-placard-staggered and motley in size as might have abutted a church in the slums. Though it was hard to read the names, Clemens could see their faint inscriptions, a rippling detail of blacks and grays that passed before his eyes and vanished. But he imagined they were peaceful names, with peaceful dead to own them.

He made his bed among the graves, book-ended by two of the taller headstones. The surrounding grass was stiff, but fragrant, and the earth, when he poked it, admitted his finger to only the first of its joints, then locked. Reclining on one elbow in his thin sleeping bag, he worked at a puzzle he had purchased in Cold Spring of a woman prostrate in a field of tall grass in front of a dark and distant house. Every time he stopped for rest he made the scene again from scratch.

Tonight he'd assembled a strata of grass, and the woman's left foot, in a lace-up gray shoe. He worked at the puzzle by the flicker and bend of a silver Zippo lighter that he carried in his shirt-front. Wedged in a crevice between embossed letters on the grave of one Lavinia Greene, the lighter had trouble sustaining itself with nothing but the shallow bronze-work to protect it, and every few minutes Clemens had to get up to re-spark the wheel when it balked in the cold. But now the flame was burning ragged. The butane, he knew, was almost out. And Clemens began to fear the dream he was working against with every puzzle. First came the dark and the dark's puzzleless-ness, then came sleep, and then the dream; but the less Clemens lay in the dark without puzzles the less chance there was of him having the dream, for it only came on in the caverns of sleep when Clemens succumbed to his constant exhaustion, when sleep closed around him like a cradling fist in which the world unmade itself. It was a dream of rebirth, and a dream of self-knowledge, and precisely for this reason, Clemens feared it profoundly. The nurse with the black void under her whites, caring for him where he lay in his bed; the nurse whose very face was an orb of pure blackness, and whose limbs had been cut from the same dark cloth, leaning in faceless and low over Clemens, performing her daubs and her ravelings. He lay there breathing vastly, the dream yet undreamt, planning his next move, eyes open. Watching his breath smoke gently, then fade. Listening to the night insects. Envisioning the puzzle-piece that would give the fallen woman in the tall grass her ankle, or the house, when he reached it, its two chimney stacks and bleak companion woodshed.

Clemens in the drugstore, searching the aisles, haggard and pale from the dream. Early morning. The proprietor was a sallow man who Clemens suspected was minding the shop with more keenness than he let on. Clemens looked at him, then away, then back, as if he had a hidden dimension. And the man was looking at him, too, with that sly and contemptible indirectness—looking at his clothes, and the dirt on his face, and the ragged carapace of his bedroll and backpack, pretending to notice everything when in truth he noticed nothing. Though Clemens never stole, the man made him nervous. People on the whole made him nervous, all kinds, appearance and demeanor aside; this was standard. So he brought a couple apples and some saltines to the counter along with ointment in a tube, and motioned high up for the man to retrieve him a yellow tin of butane. The man seemed unfamiliar with the product for a moment as he took Clemens in from head to foot.

Five dollars even, the man fired at Clemens, without once consulting his numbers.

Clemens hunted in his wallet. The man did not retrieve the tin.

I'm short, said Clemens.

To the tune of two dollars. A rubbish of pennies and thread in his pants.

Then you'll have to shop backwards, I guess, said the man. When your cash situation makes sense, I'll be here.

But I need that butane, Clemens said.

What for? said the man.

Clemens paused. For fire.

Do I look dumb to you? said the man.

Clemens assessed him: not dumb, but a hardcase. He seemed to think that Clemens was an arsonist of sorts.

I don't run this place on credit. He studied Clemens further, then grew philosophical. It all boils down to priorities really. Is it the food and the rub, or the food and the butane? The butane and rub is still out of your range.

Forget it, said Clemens. He paid for the rest.

They transacted in silence. He turned to leave.

Hey, bud, said the man. You're looking for work: try out back of the old movie theater. There's a guy named Size in an old Nissan carts spics and such around on detail. He's the one to see about money for butane. He'll pay out enough to get high for three weeks.

High? said Clemens.

Whatever you need.

I need work, said Clemens.

Okay.

This guy Size, he's hiring? said Clemens.

You could call it that, I guess.

So if I work for him, and he pays out, and I bring the money back to you, then you'll sell me that butane up there? said Clemens.

That's the idea. The man looked confused. Generally, yeah, that's how it works. But if anything changes while you're gone, I'll be sure to let you know.

The movie theater was on Main Street. Out front was a little iron maiden of a booth in which a warm body had yet to be posted, and above it a scuffed, dyslexic sign advertising in red block vinyl letters the weekday matinee. But aside from the sign, it was a street of no moment, and there were many others like it in the town, Clemens knew. Crows presided on the awnings, visiting their under-wings. Litter blew across the street the moment that the light turned green. The coagulated runoff from a three-day-old storm coursed along the gutters on its way to the Hudson. Clemens had the notion he could hear the world freezing at this early hour of its death, mid-November. Hardier men than him had perished in balmier climates than this one, he knew; he had to quit the Hudson Valley before snowfall arrived.

He walked down the alley that divided the theater from its neighbor to the west, a beer warehouse, where already men in jumpsuits were hand-trucking cases in through a speakeasy door in the back, inured to the cold, and the hour, and each other, fueled on the fact of the workday alone. They worked around Clemens and Clemens went on, nodding at them faintly, shyly. In the lot behind the theater stood three more men in what appeared to be a huddle they had formed against the cold, but when Clemens came out of the mouth of the alley he saw they were in a consultation, one of them holding a cigarette up and digging one-handed in his pocket, and the other two slapping at their coats and probing among their layered shirts. The huddle swung wide to deal with Clemens. He halfway raised a hand in greeting. The man with the cigarette wore long, dark mustaches and looked to be in his middle years. The other two men were clean-shaven and young. Clemens took the lot of them for Mexican.

Fuego? said the mustached man. He held the cigarette between his thumb and ring finger.

The other two men just stared at Clemens in endorsement of their elder's words.

Mexicans spoke Spanish, as best he recalled. This was what the man was speaking.

Clemens said simply, I don't know.

Fuego, the man said again. He mimed a lighter.

I've got one here, but it's real low. Clemens dug the Zippo from his shirt-front and proffered it.

The three men nodded their thanks, as did Clemens; but wasn't it he who had given the lighter? Why in the world was he nodding at them? Then the man lit his cigarette and snapped several drags off the end in succession, holding in a lungful against the cold air before passing on to the left.

Clemens hung back at the mouth of the alley as they lazed the cigarette between them, a half-smile forming on his face that he didn't altogether understand. He'd forgotten to ask for his Zippo back and when the men finished, the elder returned it.

Gracias, Senor, he said.

Gracias right back at you, said Clemens.

Then the three men turned around, walked to a wall that abutted the side-street and here vaulted up, one by one, to sit atop it, with their hands shoved into their shallow coat pockets. A yard or so away from them, Clemens sat against the wall, hunkered down above his bedroll, so that the mattress and sleeping bag cushioned his ribs while at the same time permitting an optimal hunch, for the burns on his back were never more painful than when he was sitting upright. The men sat in silence; their breath evanesced. Clemens slowly ate his apple. Every so often he took out the Zippo and passed it admiringly back and forth between his chapped and bloodless hands, peering at the men out of the corner of his eye, and wondering on what ground, precisely, he and the three of them stood.

Clemens was down to the core of his apple and halfway through his saltine packet when a black Nissan pickup turned down the side-street and hunted across the ruts and holes to the concrete wall at the edge of the lot; here the engine died and the fog-lights extinguished, presumably to guard the battery, and it hulked ticking there in the mid-morning cold like some dread and unpiloted vessel from Styx while the four of them looked on expectantly. The windows of the truck were tinted. For a moment nothing stirred within. A motley assortment of landscaping tools lay strewn across the bottom of the truckbed; they looked used. Clemens, at the end of the wall near the bumper, could see the Nissan's license plate, which read ENTRPNR, New Hampshire. The passenger's window labored down. A boy of nine or ten years old sat pale and uncertain near the half-open window, while a big, jowly man at the wrong end of fifty leaned across the gear-well between the cab-seats, and gestured for the three Mexicans, and then Clemens, to come and have a word. His arm, which was fit to be butchered and sold, was positioned restraint-like in front of the boy, who instantly fixed his eyes on Clemens as if he would lift it away.

Como estan, mis amigos? said the man. Tengo trabajo muy, muy especial para mis amigos a hoy. Especialmente.

Especialmente que? said the elder.

Que? said the driver. Goddamned if I know. Hablas Ingles? he said to Clemens.

I don't speak Spanish.

So it seems.

Is your name Size?

Last time I checked.

The man at the store said you're hiring for work.

I'm Theo Size and I'm hiring, he said. This is you signing the contract. Get in.

Clemens looked up and down the street, and then to the Mexicans, standing beside him. What have you got lined up? he said.

I operate on a need-to-know basis. Isn't that right, Jesus? he told the elder, who shrugged at the man, and then his fellows, but with altogether different significance. You'll see what's lined up when we get to the site.

I meant pay-wise. Lined up pay-wise. I've got to look after necessities.

Five bucks an hour before taxes, he said. Gas-money, snack-food, hydration, what not. And pay-day's on Friday, five days from today— skip town early, get no green. So what'll it be there, guy? He raised an eyebrow. Does necessity dictate you come on with us, or go squeegee cars near the onramp?

I'm coming, said Clemens. And the money sounds fine. I just wanted to think up a budget.

The three Mexicans had been clambering in while the driver and Clemens stood there talking and now the last one swung his leg over the side of the tailgate and sat. Meanwhile, the child was still staring at him from the smoke-smelling gloom of the cab.

What's your name? he said to Clemens.

That's not for you to ask, Bertrand. That's voluntary information, said Size.

My name's Clemens, Clemens said.

Cle-men-sah, enunciated the boy.

Now we're acquainted, said Size. Come aboard. He swung his big arm down the length of the tailgate as if he were trying to sell the truck used. The Mexicans sat in the truckbed and stared, not seeming to care if he came either way, waiting for him to climb in or step back with expressions of stiff early morning indifference. This job today has a timetable on it. The sooner we finish the better, I'm told. Hear that, Jesus? And he battered the ceiling. Mas rapido, mas major! Tu comprende?

The town of Ulrich rushing past: grey, post-industrial ruin. Low sun. The business district mid-refurbish: raw scaffolding, unmanned

excavations, pointless reams of orange tape. The row-house ghetto at
low boil: rusted cars gunning awake in thin driveways, lean adolescents
on all-terrain bikes, sleepless beings pale with drugs who tightrope-
walked the medians and maundered at the cafe windows, turning
to watch the truck go by with expressions of morbid half-interest.
Then strip malls, warehouses, car lots. Few passersby in between.
Stray cats. In the residential section surrounding the college life had
been given a laminate finish: sedans leaving driveways with unnatural
stealth, landscaped pets in landscaped yards, K-12 children along the
sidewalks who marked only faintly the old battered truck with the
top-heavy chassis and out-of-town plates, for in all likelihood they had
already seen it, parked outside their very homes. Size drove fast, then
slow, then fast. The assortment of shovels, picks and hoes skittered
and jounced across the truckbed. When Clemens wasn't watching
the town go by, he quietly watched the Mexicans, who perched along
the truckbed wall with their hands clamped down on the sides to
hold them upright. And every so often he studied the cab, where the
hunched silhouette of Theo Size sat with its arm around Bertrand, its
other arm compassing curves and wide turns with a steering wheel
knob altogether more suited for a Chrysler hotrod or a Chevy-Impala.

When the pickup turned east out of town on Route 80, a sour
vibration passed through Clemens. For a while he scanned the road
ahead: all of it familiar from his way into town. So maybe it was a
foreign job, nearer the Canadian border.He was just about to rap
on the window of the cab to interview Size about the site when he
saw, very faintly against the dark glass, the pale staring face of the
changeling Bertrand; it appeared to be focused on Clemens alone, as
if he alone of the men were important. The pickup turned left up a
poplar-lined drive. And then, visible through the gaps in the trees, was
the graveyard where he'd slept last night, and a half-mile beyond it, the
farmhouse.

Clemens was last to get out of the truck. He would have liked to
act natural, but still he felt nervous. Size had asked the five of them

to unload the tools from the back of the truck and follow him down among the trees, and Clemens was left there with Bertrand, who stood beside the cab-door, watching. He was dressed in a pair of grey wool slacks, a red hooded sweater and scuffed boat shoes. Clemens had thought that perhaps he was simple, but gradually saw this was not so.

He gestured at the graveyard beyond the tree-line.

A rich man wants this place dug up.

A rich man? said Clemens.

He lives in that house.

Pretty big for one guy.

I guess, said Bertrand. He's got a funny name—French, I think. I can't remember.

French from France?

Well, a Canuck, at least. But I hear they all speak it up there. It's a thing.

Why does he want it dug up? said Clemens.

Don't ask me, he said. Just does.

Clemens peered beyond the boy to where Size and the Mexicans were standing around like shabby pallbearers among the low graves.In the middle of speaking, Size looked up and gestured ostentatiously for Clemens to join them.

Where are you from?

Around, said Clemens.

My father thinks you're pretty weird.

That seems to be the consensus, all right.

Aren't you going down with the rest of those guys?

Clemens said, Probably. He rose to his feet.I just lose myself sometimes.

So I guess you could say that I found you, said the boy.

Beg pardon?

I found you. I'm the only one here.

Clemens studied him for a while, then got up. He hurdled from the bed of the truck to the ground, and his fractured ribs shifted uncomfortably. To cover the wince that he could not suppress but

44

suddenly wished to in front of the boy, Clemens bent over pretending to stretch and dusted off his smeary jeans.

Can we talk later? said the boy.

Sure, Clemens said. If I'm still here.

You mean if you don't lose yourself?

I meant gone away, said Clemens.

The boy seemed to weigh this. I hope you're around. That way we can talk some more.

Clemens nodded vaguely and began to walk on.

Keep me abreast of your plans, called the boy.

Clemens looked back on his way down the slope at the pale child standing there watching him go. He almost tripped over the first of the graves for turning around so often. Size was there to greet him at the bottom of the slope with a look of half-irate bemusement. There were bundles of shovels and gardening spades propped crutch-like beneath his arms. Clemens fetched up at the edge of the group and nodded to Size he was ready to listen.

I was just saying to the tres amigos here that we've got a situation delicado on our hands. We've got to work hard and we've got to work fast, but we've also got to work with our heads, and work careful. The Mon-suer Danielle was very clear that we keep episodes to a minimum

Why does he want it dug up? said Clemens.

Generally, I don't ask such things. Darkly irritated, Size paused to stare at him. But I'd imagine that the Mon-seur Danielle and his Missus would like a bit of peace and quiet, and maybe a front yard for their kids, if they choose to stay on here in Ulrich, that is? And I'd guess that a boneyard such as this is pretty much the opposite of scenic to them, in addition to which—and this I know—that certain of our citizens choose to ignore the legalities of Mon-seur Danielle's recent ownership. People have people buried here. Ancient ancestors, but *people*, they say. So I'd guess that the Mon-seur and Missus Danielle are tired of hosting weekly vigils for the oldest buried member of the Vanderberg clan. Can't say I blame them much myself. Me and Bertrand—who I see you've befriended—originate from out of state.

Me too, said Clemens.

Size squinted. Whereabouts?

Last I remember, Baltimore.

Last you remember? Is this guy for real? No puedes recordar de donde ere, he said. Doesn't inspire much trust, now does it, Clemens-of-possibly-Baltimore?

The Mexicans shrugged one by one in response.

It's a manner of speaking, Clemens said.

A manner of speaking. Sure, I get you. He gave a pained, sardonic smile. Frankly, though, guy, between you and me, I could care less about the place that you're from as long as you're willing to work here in this one. Because until five today, I belong to Danielle, on account of what I like to call an equitable and binding contract between gentleman. And you, Mr. Clemens, having got in my truck, are, by extension, contracted to me. As a result, whenever I speak, it's as good as the Mon-seur Danielle having spoken. So for instance when we got here, and I told you come on, help the amigos and I unload? That was the Mon-seur Danielle via Size telling you to get off your ass and help out. And the Mon-seur Danielle and his wife, Missus Inga, have the kind of good sides that you want to be on. Are you kenning me? Are we more or less straight? Do you hear words or clicks and whistles? Kindly let me know. Size breathed. I am trying to help you not fuck up.

We're straight, said Clemens.

All right—that's terrific. Just so we're all on the level, said Size. Now gentlemen. He rattled the tools. Come forward and choose your weapons.

Clemens chose a shovel with a smooth obliging grip so as to feel that he was handling the situation ably. He did not like the work, and he did not like Size, and he did not think he liked Danielle. He could see pale Bertrand through the gaps in the poplars watching them work from the hood of the truck, on the far side of which a vast tarp had been spread to be draped and cinched down on the disinterred coffins as soon as the first few were ready for transport. It would all be a matter

46

of transport, said Size, who took pains to distinguish between this and grave-robbing for the benefit of Clemens and the Mexicans both, and so they made work of one plot at a time while Size supervised from on top of a headstone. When their shovels struck wood, they shouldered the coffin through the thin screen of trees between the graveyard and the driveway, and covered it beneath the tarp before going back to refill in the holes. Last they set into the placard or headstone to be placed in the truck in advance of the coffin. Then with the works huddled under the tarp, they drove the truck across the road to a clearing not deep in the forest of cedars, where they buried the coffins and dug in the markers with an eye for recreating their arrangement in the field. Size had traced a blueprint so immediate kin would not find themselves next to strangers.

But it all proved easier said than done. Digging up graves was an art or a science that none of the men, Size included, were versed in. The top layer of earth was hard, and its substrata viscous with cold, like an ice floe, but the further and further the four of them dug the more diverse the gravesite's character—by turns dark and crumbly, or armored in slate, or clayey and slick as a ditch in a downpour, due to which, finally, Clemens fell, sprawled on his back with a laugh of surprise, and the younger of the work-crew had to toggle him out with the dull business-ends of their shovels. The fall was awful on his burns, which he felt re-inflaming and weeping anew beneath his mud-encumbered flannel. And the digging was more of the same on his ribs, a blunt and reverberant southerly pain in the cavernous space of his abdomen. Size watched the fall and recovery both with a sardonic glee from on top of his headstone. But beyond a headshake and the words, Oh Christ, he offered no encouragement. The Mexicans worked dutifully, and were no more forthcoming than they had been before, but Clemens sensed in them when removed from Size's presence if only by a distance of fifteen feet a trace of the old gregariousness they had shown in the parking lot early that morning; in the way they moved their limbs less stiffly, in the wry bits of Spanish they bandied about, in the way they had smiled and laughed with Clemens as they dragged him up out of the hole. When their shovels struck wood in the work day's third plot, Clemens and the Mexicans took up positions each one to a corner on the half-exposed casket, and then with the trough-ends they levered it up until they were able to lift with their hands. Then, breathing curses and fighting for traction, they started to move it toward the light. But one of the bearers lost his footing—Clemens thought the elder of the Mexicans, Jesus—and the coffin went tobogganing back through the mud and slammed into the grave's far wall, the impact of which sent its lid flapping open on the side of the box nearest Clemens. An instance of lining the shade of old blood, the ruins of a white dress-shirt, but nothing of the wearer save a long skein of grey, which might or might not have been hair. The lid closed.

Goddamn it, said Size from the top of the hole. Let's not hasten nature's work.

The four of them stood for a moment in silence above the remains of William Rindt.

Around two o'clock a Ford Fairlane in peppermint green pulled into the drive, and a long-legged woman in a waitress uniform who looked to be in her early forties approached the graveyard from the road. She carried a large paper sack in her hands, and it looked bottom-heavy with grease. There was a light asymmetry to her features—the right eye bigger than its sister, and her sun-cured neck was very long, with a handsome knob of throat. Clemens watched her. Two of the graves had been exhumed and relocated to the woods as per instructions, but there were eighteen in all and the men were exhausted. As the woman came on, the four of them rested. Everyone knew, including Clemens, that the project would herald a shit-show unceasing without a CAT to help them dig. Clemens leaned against the grave where his feet had been pressed the night before, his headboard having been removed along with the day's second coffin. Bertrand, who'd come down from the truck, haunted Clemens, waiting to be addressed or shooed. The long-throated woman slipped in through the poplars and heeled down the slope towards the men in her flats.

Size announced, The lady Carol. Come on now, pick up your pants. A woman of class is among you. Observe her.

The woman named Carol walked over the graves to where Clemens leaned with Bertrand at his side, and placed the paper sack on the bronze-embossed tablet where he had had his lighter wedged. She scanned Clemens from head to toe and did not seem hugely impressed, but a rushing back behind her eyes revealed she had a complex opinion. The eyes were bright green, out of true in circumference, the left one larger than the right. What did they say about left versus right—which one was the better direction? thought Clemens. He might be yet a handsome man, or anyway, he thought, not ugly. But his travels had been scarce of mirrors and he was conscious of the rawness of his unexamined face.

Twenty-five fifty, the lady told Size. Four pastrami melts, a BLT, and a hotdog for Bertrand. Plus delivery.

Got change for forty? Size said.

She nodded. Size began to dig in his wallet for bills.

She turned to the foul, recumbent Clemens. You're new, she observed of the tramp. Are you named?

Bertrand said: He's Clemens.

He said it, said Clemens.

Really, she said, smiling down at Bertrand. Can the son of Theo Size be trusted? Clemens looked the woman in the eyes, then away. So far he can. Just likes to talk.

So he talks to you, too?

Yes, Ma'am.

And you answer?

He peered at her. Sometimes I do.

Where are you from, Mr. Clemens? she said.

Somewhere I don't think you know.

 I hope you like yourself a Reuben.

It's the rich man who wants them dug up, said Bertrand.

The woman said to Clemens, Are you aware of the controversy?

Clemens shook his head. I just got here last night.

I thought you were from Baltimore. Size loped over the stones, cash in hand. Clemens' face darkened. Like I said, one of many.

Many what? Carol said.

Many places, said Size. Mister Clemens here is a regular Magellan. How do you think he got so pretty?From sleeping en suite at the Ritz every night?

He just needs a bath, she said. Theo, pay this man in soap.

It's not my prerogative to dapper his dan. I just need him conscious.

What about the rest of you guys? she said. She nodded to the Mexicans who hadn't been listening or bothering to understand. Un jefe bueno, eso hombre, Theo Size?

They shrugged their shoulders one by one.

From three Mexicans, that's a blessing, said Size. Crooks in alleys, crooks on high. All they know is crooks. Not me.

They gave their answer, said the woman. And when have you given a shit what they think? As for you, Clemens. She knelt down beside him and flicked a dirt clot from the toe of his sneaker. Come down to my place for that bath if you want. Corner of Till and Raymond street. I'll hose you off with the grill around closing.

Thanks, said Clemens. I just might.

We appreciate you taking the time, said Size. We appreciate you for who you are.

Carol started uphill.

What a woman she is. A miraculous woman, Size said, on a grin.

Yet a lifelessness haunted the foreman's expression as he watched her ascend the small hill toward her car.

Clemens watched Size. She's nice all right.

She sure took a bright shine to you, said Size.

She pities me mostly, said Clemens. That's all.

Meanwhile, Bertrand had got hold of the sack and begun to distribute the sandwiches. The Mexicans ate slowly, talking in between mouthfuls. Size spread the halves of his sandwich partway, shook the bacon free and chewed. His eyes never left his son Bertrand as the boy made his way round to Clemens.

I saved this one for you, he said. It's got a good weight and it smells super strong. He cradled the sandwich for Clemens to see. I'll bet it's the best of the four, he assured.

He nodded his thanks to the boy and unwrapped it. Bertrand stood there and watched him eat. The day was at its warmest.

By nine that night, he was back in the graveyard, lying in his sleeping bag, working on the puzzle. He'd only left the site that evening for the benefit of Size and the rest of the crew when he'd ridden to town in the pickup again to playact at renting a room for himself at a motor hotel just east of downtown. Clemens had then retraced his steps along the back-roads where he wouldn't be seen and had waited in the woods across the way from Danielle's property until the sky bruised in his favor. Then camped. Now he was sprawled on his hip in the grass with a tired arm propped under his chin for support, swirling puzzle-pieces across the bronze marker, looking for matches among the unmatched. But Clemens could not see too well; his gloveless fingers fumbled things. He'd begun to feel senile with cold as he lay there, and had considered taking shelter in Danielle's barn only to think better of it every time. He had the woman in the puzzle halfway pieced together from the soles of her old-fashioned shoes moving up, with her legs and rump defined against a faded pink dress beside which a hand, disembodied from the rest of her, supported her listing torso upright, while the tall grass around her was darkening slightly the closer he came to assembling the house. The actual house upon the hill was still aglow with yolky light. Only birds and bats astir. Then, a sudden human presence. The lights of Carol's Ford Fairlane fencing in between the poplars before they died away again when the car shunted left up the driveway and stopped. He had heard the car coming, but nothing of Carol; slowly, the deficit started to spook him. But then he saw her wading through the roadside fog and passing through the screen of poplars in a long, tan coat belted tight at the waist with her hair gathered up in a scarf, arms extended. She seemed to be feeling her way through the fog or pursuing some uncanny instinct beyond her, and Clemens reflected on vampires and zombies, denizens of graveyard earth, the thought of them now proving comforting, strangely, like benevolent guardians on this, their home turf.

She said not a word to the cemetery-dweller until she was standing above him.

Dinner, she said. Since you passed up the bath.

She held a bag much like the one she'd brought lunch in.

Thank you, said Clemens. I didn't feel dirty.

Considering where you make your bed, somehow that doesn't surprise me.

She knelt.

How did you know I was here? he said.

Just a guess, really. It's dark here, and quiet. Also, it's free and a place that you know. Lucky for me, it was just the one guess—this is the first place I went looking.

Clemens snapped the Zippo shut to ration what butane remained for the puzzle, and the dark came upon them so wholesale and sudden it almost made him gasp out loud.

Carol's eyes sought Clemens' in a cloud-break of moonlight that fell on the graves.

I'll be frank. I like you Clemens. I like how you look, and the things that you say. Now I want to know… And her palm brushed his cheek. What would you do if I climbed in there with you?

I'm kind of in the middle of something, said Clemens. He nodded at the puzzle of the woman in the field. Maybe for a minute or two. To keep warm.

She looked at him sternly, extended herself and wriggled feet first into the sleeping bag beside him. Clemens hadn't been with a woman in eons. He had no idea what to do. Carol pressed herself against him. She smelled like soap and kitchen grease. She hadn't taken off her shoes and he could feel the roughness of them through the holes in his socks.

Carol whispered, Christ, you smell.

I'm used to it, I guess, said Clemens.

She guided his hand through the V of her coat and it must've been warm, she was bare underneath it. She started to kiss his bearded cheek and made him commit to discovering her breast. He pressed his nose into the crown of her head, dwelt for a time in her hair, found it suited him. Then she kissed him on the lips, modulating pressure, duration, and speed; he thought she kissed erratically, unpredictably, schizophrenically, but was yet unaware of other ways to go about it. When at last she cupped his groin in the palm of her hand, he startled and jolted away from her.

Too much? Carol said.

Clemens shrugged in the darkness. This is all pretty new to me.

Don't tell me you haven't.

I have. In the past. But that was all that Clemens said.

You mean you don't remember?

I probably have.

How can you not remember *that*?

Clemens shook his head, squirmed a little in the bag. His face was gloaming over with indifference, and she saw it.

Hey. She shook him lightly. Hey, Clemens. Stay with me. She shook him again. Come back to me now.

I'm sorry, he said. Can I just lie here?

I'm not going anywhere.

Can we just lie here, then? For now.

By way of an answer, she shifted aside and wrapped herself around him like a garment.

But Carol dozed before too long, and Clemens was left to contend with dream. He had thought that the fact of her presence alone would be enough to stave it off, but when the dream welled like a gout of dark water from some vast and unspeakable reservoir in him, Clemens had worked too hard that day to turn his back on rest. The same shadow-being in the same nurse's whites emerged from the blackness of sleep to greet Clemens, though he no longer feared the nurse, it was the nurse who now feared him, and she seemed to approach and retreat from him both in a strange sort of wavering dance against nature, her arms reaching out to lay a blessing on Clemens, or maybe to hold him at bay. Then he woke. Carol lay beside him in the closeness of the bag, her coat and shoes still on, eyes closed. It was somewhere in the neighborhood of just before dawn. Crows along the headstones and the branches of the poplars watched the lovers stirring out of cold, sagacious eyes.

Nightmares, she said through the fan of her hair. You've been peddling your feet like a dog through the night.

Sorry I woke you, said Clemens. It's early.

She yawned up at him. I was already up.

They climbed out of the sleeping bag and sat in the winter-scorched grass, coming to. Then, without much conversation, they ate the cold chicken for breakfast.

Mid-morning that day Danielle came down to see how the work-crew was getting along. He was dressed fussily, like a gentleman farmer, in a loose linen suit meant to lend him forbearance, and on his feet, the cold be damned, a pair of brocade slippers. He was short, with close-set shoulders, and a muscular chest—push-ups on the bedroom floor, a military man, or an athlete. In spite of his build he smoked heavy Gauloises with cursory, impatient pulls. Bertrand had come down from the hood of the truck to watch this surveying unfold.

Though Clemens was standing too far from the men to hear exactly what they said, he could tell that Danielle was displeased in some capacity, and that Size, many-smiled, had been leveraging his faith. The Mexicans had retired their tools at the edge of their latest excavation, which was already their second go at exhuming the body of Eustace Greene. His headstone was planted ten steps west of where the body actually lay and required that the men dig two separate holes, the first of which they had filled in, so that the morning had consisted, to Size's dismay, of exhuming a tenantless plot with manpower that tended to wane around five o'clock. Clemens' burns were acting up, and his two trick ribs hadn't fared much better after the night he'd spent nesting with Carol. Digging graves in the cold against time with no tractor was highly inappropriate work.

He was in pain.

Twice already that morning he had had to stop digging and stand hunched over the dirt close to nausea, and the three Mexicans had stopped working in turn to lean on their tools in a circle around him, asking in Spanish what was wrong; and yet it was all he could do just to mime that this was a brief episode and would pass, but still they stood there, scared for Clemens, patting him searingly on the back, calling to Size, Enfermo! Enfermo!, pointing at him with wide brown eyes as if he were, finally, Eustace Greene, risen up in the full flush of death, begging water.

Size had responded, Let him breathe. He's just afraid of the dark. Back to work.Bertrand walked up, tugged Clemens' sleeve.

He's shorter than I thought he'd be.

He certainly is compact, said Clemens.

Are you all right?

So-so, said Clemens.

You look like you're in pain.

A little.

What's the difference? Pain is pain.

Clemens watched him, said: I guess.

One minute I'm sorry for you, said Bertrand. And the next minute I think you're brave.

Clemens was silent. Okay, he responded.

—half-assed funerals, Size was saying. Fool townfolk of yesteryear. Barring you wanting them moved off your land, they'd endanger your health before too long. Decomposition. Fuck all of a thing. Contaminates the drinking water. Man in Poughkeepsie some years back that built his house behind a parish. Got his water from a reservoir near there too. And the damndest thing was—

The men stopped walking. Clemens and Bertrand stood together like conspirators. Size's eyes flicked with a gunner's precision between the young tramp and his son. Danielle, who was probably just checking up, rocked back and forth on his heels.

Clear out, son. This is stockholders only. Bertrand hastened off through the trees toward the truck. Size said of Clemens, He's a goldbricker, this one. So little self-respect. Sad, really.

He's been through the wringer, all right, said Danielle. Just who are you employing here?

The rich man's voice was accent-less. He might have come from California. Whoever I can, said Size. He's able. But that's a legitimate question.

Claude Danielle, said Danielle, hand extended.

Clemens did not move to take it.

Come on, he said. Forget the dirt. I don't employ unshaken hands.

By inches, Clemens took the hand. It was soft, and the suit-cuff was soiled upon contact.

Pleased to meet you, said the rich man. Keep up the pace and we'll think on a bonus. He made to start wiping his hands on his pants but seeing their bright pleatedness he stopped short, and clasping them, hiding the dirt, he walked on, insisting to Size as they went down the graves that he make the acquaintance of all the work crew, and so engaged them, one by one, to the wincing apprehension of the foreman.

Size addressed them, Take a break. The Mon-seur Danielle has got something to tell us.

Mister Danielle is just fine, said the rich man. I was raised in Montreal. Now Theo, I want you to translate my words for these gentlemen of Hispanic descent. I want them to know the indispensable service they're doing both me and my wife.

I'll try my best.

He mumbled Spanish. The Mexicans nodded their heads dubiously.

There are people buried here, he said. That fact we can all agree on. But the truth underlying the fact, as I see it, is that people have to live here, too—people still among the living, people, in short, with priorities. I never asked you to deface their headstones, or to pose with them for pictures, or to piss in their coffins. All that I'm asking—from you, from this town—is to let a man live on his spread undisturbed. I paid for this land, this house, and this graveyard, and I paid for my privacy right along with it. And in the scheme of things, gentleman, what have we done but move a few holes a few yards west? Easier on the dead, you'd think, than lying in disputed ground, having to listen to squabbles, and shouts, and local news people with cameras and booms, when they could be just across the road, in a sun-dappled clearing, at peace. I won't ask you to like the work. I won't ask you to like the wages. But I will ask you to take the time to understand the man who hired you. I'm telling you this in a generous spirit. You have reservations. This I know. What Christian man wouldn't have reservations? But if someone came snooping, for instance, today, and hit on the four of you digging out here, I'd ask you to impress on him the gist of what I just told you. Danielle met the eight pairs of eyes one by one with a smile trembling on his lips, then a finger. Utmost decorum is called for here. But I'm sure that you already knew that, he said.

Size had been struggling to translate Danielle, let alone pronounce the words, and Clemens deduced by the pace he was speaking that he was somewhere in the neighborhood of Danielle's introduction. The Mexicans were nodding their heads to continue, though it was clear they were both irritated and confused.

I basically see what you're saying, said Clemens.

The Canadian nodded. Then you're all right by me.

Size, who'd forsaken his bilingual flailings, approached Danielle and took his arm as if to escort him off the site but not before telling the congress of men: The customer makes his own standards. Our motto. Thank the Mon—Mister Danielle for his time.

Thank you, said Clemens.

The Mexicans nodded.

It was a pleasure to meet you boys, said Danielle.

He lit another smoke, then, from the ruin of the prior and stood for a time with his hand cupped around it until the burning end took up. Whereupon, about-facing, his linen suit rippling, like some sharecropping gentry of old on parade, he high-stepped slowly up the hill exuding a thinness of smoke from his head. Clemens felt a hand touch the back of his shoulder and turned around sure he would find Bertrand lurking. But it was Carol who stood there, contained in her coat, cradling another lunch for six against her stomach.

Mister Clemens, she said.

Clemens nodded once, slowly, and then as slowly turned away.

It seems that I just missed your great benefactor.

Mon-se-ur my ass, said Size.

Food's up, Senor Pit Boss.

She rattled the lunches.

Size said: Huh. He turned around.

Carol's face softened. For heaven's sake, Theo. A little fatter in the wallet, so he tosses it around.

Size looked at Carol, then Clemens, the group. Bertrand had been riding the edge of the hood while straining forward rigidly to see through the poplars, but now he must have strained too far because he slid from the top and goose-stepped out of sight.

To hell with it then, said Size. Let's eat. But it's digging double-time for the rest of the day. Mister Danielle of Montreal is expecting this ground cleared out by Sunday.

You doing all right, Mr. Clemens? said Carol.

But Clemens had nothing to say on that score.

At the end of the day, Clemens stood by the truck, digging in his backpack for the lavender trinket, which he always refastened as soon as his shovel rang down among the others in the truckbed at five. The Mexicans stood some yards away, sharing a Lucky drag for drag. Bertrand was in the passenger's seat of the pickup, where he'd been remanded by Size after lunch, a pale fuzzy, humanoid shape through the windows, like an ectoplasm caught on film. Clemens felt a massiveness behind him: Theo Size.Lifelong smoker's equine breathing. Bulk of him stealing over Clemens in grotesque negative on the grass.

I'll bet ladies like the smell. I'll bet Carol does, he said.

It keeps me on my toes, said Clemens.

Keeps your pecker hard, you say?

When Clemens turned around, Size laughed.

Does she screw like a waitress, a widow, or both? Haven't had the pleasure yet, but I'm one of few in this town. Ask around.

That doesn't sound like my business, said Clemens.

Size looked Clemens up and down with a tilted, uncomfortable smile. She's found a forgiving man in you. Most women would be so lucky. But permit me to ask: do you screw her right here or do you save it for that half-star hotel where you're staying? Not that she's above it, mind you.

It's not the way you think it is.

What way is it, then? said Size.

And with that he got into the cab of the truck without giving Clemens a chance to respond. He whistled for the Mexicans to hop in the back, which they managed to do much faster than Clemens, and when the truck began to roll he was forced into awkward pursuit to catch on, calling to Size, The breaks! The breaks! but he just started gunning for road, trailing Clemens while the graveyard became a vertiginous smear in the sudden, accelerant wake of the engine. The Mexicans pulled him aboard and he thanked them. He watched Size driving into town, taking broad turns of a wishful destruction, eyeing the rearview with paranoid stealth as if to gauge the motives of his passengers. At some point Bertrand must have said something to him that Size in his rage could not abide because his huge, butcher's parcel of an arm swung out and caught the pale boy on the side of the head. But scarcely had the arm recoiled than it rose again in consolation and held Bertrand close for the rest of the ride as he wept in muffled tones beyond the window.

He waited for Carol that night on a headstone, the puzzle unexamined at his feet; he was hungry. The cold had formed for him a dreadful affinity, and one he could suffer all night and not shake unless he stood to jog a bit and get his circulation going, though it did little more than remind his stiff limbs how vastly indisposed they were. The lights of Danielle's house were out. Carol's car pulled up the drive. Clemens thought to roll out his bag in the grass, but was unsure of what that would mean for the two of them. At the top of the hill, Carol passed through the poplars, walked down the slope and across the wet grass, but stopped a bit short of where Clemens was standing, and backed playfully towards the trees.

Come and walk with me, she said.

Where are we going? said Clemens.

Exploring.

Clemens reached for his backpack at the base of the grave.

Leave that here, she said. Come on.

Clemens sat watching her. Then rose again. She waited for him at the edge of the light like a comely ferrywoman or a shepherdess. When Clemens fell in step beside her, mounting toward the long, dark house, she took his arm in hers—firmly—and promenaded in the lead. He enjoyed the sinew of her, and the heat she gave off, and the careful quickness of her tread; how she grabbed at his arm with her one free hand in spite of the fact that she already held it.

You know, his wife is barely twenty. Carol pointed at the house. He got her off a cow farm in Europe, I hear. Switzerland, Germany, Austria, maybe—someplace the girls are all chesty and blonde. Never comes to town with him. Never leaves the house at all. And the only reason I know that is because of the hubbub attached to this graveyard. Paper's been hounding that man and his wife since he first brought it up at a town hall meeting, and then, a week later, with no one on board, he dropped a petition on the county. But when they went ahead and put a cork in that too by tying it up in the zoning law courts, well, he decided it was time. With or without their approval, she said. But no one in Ulrich fears the worst unless it's a factory shutdown, or weather. That's what allows you hardheads to keep working: the fundamental decency of people towards people. And anyway, it's been too cold for people to visit their dead. She sighed. Flowers in this weather turn into blown glass the minute they touch the air. I've seen it. But what about you? I do go on. Stand with me a second. Listen.

They'd more than halfway crossed the field, and were standing on a level with the darkened farmhouse.

What are we listening for? said Clemens.

I don't hear a thing, he said.

That's the sound I mean, she said. Doesn't it make you want to scream? To call out, Stop, I haven't been listening, I haven't been living at all, I've been deaf.

Shhh, he said, indicating the house. This isn't the place or time to scream.

Let's push on, she said.

Clemens balked.

Aren't you having fun? she said.

You're acting...strange.

Oh, am I now? And who are you to say I'm acting?

Clemens looked hopelessly away from the question.

I'm flirting with you, said Carol. Okay? I'm nervous, and I flirt when I'm nervous—I *flirt*. Haven't you ever been nervous?

He nodded.

And what do you do?

He was silent a moment. The opposite of you, said Clemens.

Within twenty yards of Danielle's house, a light on the ground floor startled on, and its lateral twin fell over the grass just below the window. Nothing stirred or sounded there. Then a shape passed by the glass.

Who do you think that was? said Carol.

I couldn't get a read on the gender, said Clemens.

A read, she said. The way you talk. She kissed him on the cheek, like a spritz of warm water. Let's get a little bit closer.

No thanks.

We can see them, they can't see us.

I know how it works, said Clemens. No thanks.

I'm going, she said. Here I go. Try and stop me. She started to creep round the side of the house. Unless you come and peep-tom with me, I'm pressing my face to the glass, she said. Clemens hesitated. Here goes, she said. Pressing, pressing. Closer, closer.

He walked over briskly. Okay, you can stop.

I knew this light was going to suit you.

Indirect light.

Soft light, she amended. But you look just as good at high noon, in a grave.

The shape traversed the room again too fast for them to see its face, but its hair was blonde and shoulder length, its figure petite and softly made and it trailed in its wake like benign ectoplasm a pale blue cotton nightgown.

Must be her, said Carol. The wife.

Clemens stared in silence at the empty square of light. The room had a raw, nervous aspect in her absence, as if by passing through it she had set it on edge.

The woman reappeared by the table in her gown. She looked as young as people said, but in her movements much, much older. She raised the green mug to her lips and drank of it, and her young woman's breasts pressed the front of her gown and she held the green mug in both hands for a moment to feel the warmth of it before setting it down. Then she disappeared again, footsteps shaking the pane in its casement.

What do you think she's doing? said Clemens.

You say that like you have no clue.

You're sorry for her.

I was her once.

Where's your husband now?

Long dead.

Clemens looked at Carol sheepishly. He could not read her. Her face was half in shadow, half in light.

While he was off dying, I walked all night. We had a house then, much smaller than this one, but still big enough to take a turn or two in. And come early morning when I got into bed, he would see I was tired, and he would see I was fretful, and he would see that he was all there was. But he never asked me, Carol, where have you been? Why do you walk the way you do? Why don't you come to bed now, Carol? I want you in bed, right here, with me. Since then, I've known a lot of men. I'm not ashamed to tell you that. You didn't have to tell me.

No, I didn't, said Carol. But here we are a couple seconds later. And you know.

Some minutes later, back in the graveyard, Clemens excused himself to piss, and while he was gone she had gotten undressed, snuck into his sleeping bag and she lay there while twitching her nose for the cold with the ends of her hair trailing over her shoulders. He stood above her for a time, searching his pockets for items unknown.

You don't need to use a rubber. I've got a clean bill of health, she said.

I wasn't looking for one, said Clemens. I was just digging around to kill time.

Carol smiled at him. Come lie here with me.

Clemens peeled off his pants. Okay. Then he winced out of his flannel and shirt and stood trembling in the dark in his naturals. And then, standing there, he began to grow hard with the sheer novelty of his predicament.

I want you, said Carol. Please come here.

Clemens knelt down, shucked the bag and got in.

Carol told Clemens, You're my favorite. Did you know that?

He looked bemused. Your favorite what?

But she didn't specify, just started in kissing, with the same senselessness as before, which he welcomed. And Clemens felt good knowing he was her favorite, not knowing why or due to what or out of what body of lesser contenders, only that he bore this title, and now must endeavor to own it. So he reached for Carol in the dark to properly express his thanks, but before he could touch her, she was wetting herself and guiding him in between her legs, and she gave a sharp sigh as the gap closed between them and continued to sigh as he nosed in her hair. For a while he did not move his hips, so Carol urged him on with hers, at the same time pulling him further inside her by every handhold she could find on his back. She was a lean ferocity of breath within the confines of the bag; he could not have refused what she wanted to give, even had he tried to. But then Carol froze, as if Clemens, in heat, had whispered unspeakable things in her ear. Though in truth she'd discovered the snakeskin of burns that covered a fourth of his back.

These are pretty fresh, she said.

Please, not now, said Clemens. Please.

A halfway house in Baltimore. That's where I woke up, said Clemens.

They were lying in the sleeping bag, mellow and damp.

The burns on my back were much worse then. I could hardly stand to piss. And two of my ribs were broke. Still are.

You don't seem that broke to me.

Clemens smiled at Carol. To you, maybe, yeah. But my back and my ribs, they like to act up. They like to remind me who I am. It's like they belong to the guy that I was but that death couldn't quite put the freeze on.

The guy you were?

There was a woman, he said. A nurse in the house where I was.

Your friend.

Clemens shook his head. No, it wasn't like that. She tended to me for three weeks in that hole. They'd brought me in like that, three guys.

Tell me they were friends of yours.

That's the thing, he said. Didn't know them. Couldn't even tell you what they looked like. Just guys. They dropped me on the curb one night, all burned to hell, with my ribs busted up. But I didn't have to ask that nurse to know they were the wrong kinds of guys to be with— bad guys, evil guys, you could tell by her face. By the way she came into my room, tiptoeing. By the way she never touched me with her fingers directly, always through the cloth she was wrapping around.

So let me get this straight, said Carol. You were in some kind of fight?

Sure, some kind of fight. He shrugged. I was on the losing side.

But why take you there, to that house? she said. Why not somewhere they could treat you?

Whatever I was mixed up in, that house was the only place for it, he said. Those guys that brought me in that night, they must've been tougher than hell—real convincers. Or else they must've been in funds. Tell me what kind of halfway house would take a damage case like me.

A place for drunks.

And needle-men.

Not for the critical cases, said Carol. But was it all that bad? Were you?

I was doped from dawn to dawn. But it's not the pain I remember, said Clemens. It was how she looked at me, that nurse. Like she was scared of where I'd been. Because the state I was in, all burned up and broken—why would she be scared of me? No wallet. No shoes. No tags on my clothes. Scrubbed clean, as they say. A ghost. And she was the one scared of me—more than scared. It was a reckoning she was on. She despised me.

Maybe she was Mormon, then.

No, said Clemens. It wasn't religious. It had nothing to do with religion at all. But it was human, I guess. I disgusted her, maybe. She couldn't seem to help the way she felt in my presence. No matter how beat I might've looked. No matter how nice I was to her—it was like... And here he groped for words, casting his hands above the bag. It was like, any minute, I'd turn, he said. Back into the guy I'd been before. That whatever I'd suffered, it wasn't enough. She would never understand it, that nurse, never trust me. She was my world for three weeks. Three weeks. She was as good as my mother.

Clemens felt something blaze in him with the venom of an angry wire. He worked his jaw convulsively, willing it to fasten on the words he would speak, but all he did was bite his tongue and the metal taste welled in his mouth, without pain.

A man as busted up as you, and he gets the high-and-mighty from a girl—a little girl. Oh Clemens, said Carol, slowly shaking her head. You were better off not knowing.

But not the way you think, said Clemens. After a while, it wasn't her that got to me. I could tell what she thought of me just by looking, and nothing she said would've been a surprise. But whoever I was before that night when they brought me in all burned and busted— some guy with a name that was different than mine, some guy with a past that was different, a future—well, I didn't want to know anymore who he was. Not after I saw what it did to that nurse. No more than I want to know now, he said, about the guy I am.

Carol took his face in her hands. You're Clemens. You're Clemens, she repeated. And I love you to death.

You don't mean that and you know it.

Let's just go to sleep, she said. If you're going to do this, let's just sleep.

This time he felt the anger boil at the pity and the sentimental foolishness in her, but it came too fast for him to harness, so he let it simmer over into silence. Then they lay there.

Clemens, she said. Please give me your arms.

And he gave them to her because she'd asked, not having any excuse but to give them. And Carol clung to him in a vise of thin arms, trembling a bit in her curl up against him, as if Clemens, bruised and battered though she knew him to be, were the last purchase-point on a fall from great heights.

Because life had begun in the dingy room with the terrified nurse standing over his bed, Clemens climbed out from her arms an hour later and started to work at the puzzle. The moon was bright enough that he did not need the lighter and Clemens felt blessed in that respect, but what about the next night, with a skinnier moon and the puzzle more than halfway finished? And what about the next night? The night after that? Nights now past and nights to come and nights that might or might not be, the accumulate baffling nothingness of them, but also a something-ness, too, and this worse. He sifted through the puzzle shards for the bent and emaciate arm of the woman, and when he had found it, the rest of her dress, all the way up to her dark head of hair, which trailed a couple wiry strands that he knew to look for against a backdrop of orange since the grass to either side of her was darker than the pale, yellow kind near the house. Then before long Clemens had her whole cloth, and soon the field of grass around her. Next came the house, and to the west of it the woodshed, until at last from what remained Clemens assembled the sky. Meanwhile the sky above the actual field was beginning to look a lot like dawn, and the crows had departed, succeeded by thrushes. Clemens watched Carol who slept without stirring, all but her shoulders cocooned in the bag. And she began to seem to him like somebody he'd seen in passing: a face he'd half glimpsed on some sidewalk at dusk, or a profile gliding past him in the sections of a train. It was the kind of seeing her that could happen but once, and when it was done he felt tired.

He left her sleeping there alone and walked uphill past Danielle's house. He headed for a stand of elms and gauging the height of the tallest he climbed, upwards and upwards and hand over hand across the bald and crooked limbs, until he arrived at the top, a sort of cradle, and hung his legs to rest. From up there the whole of the field could be seen, and the back of the house, and the dark stretch of road, and the early morning traffic in a sinuous blur between the interstices of the trees. But Clemens watched the graveyard at the bottom of the hill. Dawn was complicating things. He could just make out the shape of Carol sprawled in his bag among the stones. From on top of the hill, he watched her rise, a small, black shape jackknifing upright, shifting and yawning, orienting itself. He doubted he could call her name, or motion to her, had he wanted to. But Clemens could hear her calling him. Her voice was shrill with thwarted love. Her voice was shrill with many things, but thwarted love foremost among them, and not thwarted then, when she didn't see Clemens and couldn't find him when she looked, but thwarted before there was something to thwart, before love itself, or before there was Clemens. Still inside the sleeping bag, holding it up beneath her chin, she started to shuffle through the graves, calling his name more urgently, beginning to hop, then, to cover more ground, at first toward the road before swinging around in a wide, hopping turn like a spry amputee, and moving instead toward the base of the hill, but with too much momentum to slow herself down, due to which she tripped and sprawled and lay for a time in the bag, unmoving. Then she emerged in the nude from the bag, and walked across the freezing grass, and stopped among the graves to look at something near her feet. In a rage too far for him to hear, Carol fell to kicking his puzzle to pieces, breasts jostling with the strain. Then she dressed. When Clemens came down in the wake of her Ford to hastily gather his camp for the day, the puzzle lay strewn in a raw constellation five feet in every direction.

When Theo Size drove up that day to take the four Mexicans and Clemens to work, he called from the front, Hey Clemens. Get in, while the other four men vaulted up into the truck bed. He sat where Bertrand would've normally sat had he been in the car, but he wasn't. Size did not speak for a long stretch of time as he piloted the pickup along the cold roads, just kept smoking, butt by butt, fouling the air of the cab. When Clemens attempted to roll down the widow, Size reached out and stayed his hand.

Bertrand's run off on me, he said. MIA since yesterday.

Any idea where to? said Clemens

If I knew that—well, hell, said Size. Hence the expression run off?

He smiled darkly.

All I meant was, boys have haunts. Thought maybe you'd know Bertrand's, said Clemens.

Size smoked in silence, a continuous drag, and the body of his ash grew longer. You say that like someone who knows, he said. Like someone with haunts of his own. Like a spook.

Did you ask me up here to get my opinion, or make your own ring truer? said Clemens.

The foreman was silent a moment too long. They're pretty bound up in my mind at the moment.

The two men watched the road advance. Clemens fiddled with his Zippo. A revelation came to Size and he slapped the steering wheel with the flat of his palm.

Hey now, he said. I don't mean to offend. But a man's got to ask when it comes to his own. And you know what? You're probably right. About Bertrand, I mean—his haunts. Boys have *haunts*. You said that, right?

I'm sure Bertrand's somewhere, said Clemens.

Buddy o' mine, said Theo Size, I like the kind of straight you talk. He cranked the window suddenly to pitch the vanquished Lucky out, and a turbulent in-suck of late autumn air went dervishing all through the cab, drawing smoke. Just hearing you say those words, just now, I'm pretty goddamned sure myself.

The four of them digging in a plot for many hours without woodfall, while Size oversaw from the lip of the grave with the smoke from his Luckies getting sucked away windward, butt after butt rolling down the dirt walls to extinguish in the water that was welling at the bottom. Jesus found the ones with tobacco still in them to be smoked later on in the post-lunch hours when Size had finished off his pack, and this he would do at the rate he was smoking. The three youngbloods stared up at him, hard about the eyes. Yet if Size was not liked, he had noticed it hardly. The man had eyes for Clemens only. And his was a churning and low-minded stare, with a strange innocence at the core of it. Lavinia Greene's casket was nowhere in sight, the same as her brother Eustace Greene's. Apparently, the family had migrated in damp, or been buried out of sequence long ago. When Clemens' shovel got lost in deep mud and sucking free suddenly threw him back, Size shouted down for the men to stop digging and take a stock of where they were.

Burrow like gophers if you have to. Just find her.

The idea did not appeal to anyone.

Among the haggard, sweaty men who dug with blood beneath their nails was the notion of somehow being toyed with, foot by empty foot.

Clemens was attempting to communicate in Spanish the risks of digging sideways through a wall of loose dirt, miming a fatal collapse with his hand while repeating a word he had seen on street signs, *pelgro* instead of *peligro.*

Well, give it a go anyway, said Size. I'll be right here with the backhoe.

Clemens just shrugged, and raised his shovel, and pried out a chunk of the wall with the trough. The dirt underwent a convulsion. All jumped. A clayey dust infused the air. Then, as Clemens leaned in close, a gout of dirt erupted forth, and the coffin came shuttling through the earth like something in a funhouse chute, burst through a veil of roots and dirt and settled on its side.

Man alive, said Size, still laughing. They dug the girl in at a slant. That's fantastic.

Help me with this thing, said Clemens, recruiting the help of all four hands. And the four of them tipped the casket up and stood around it coughing.

An hour before lunch, with the coffin transported, the hole reinterred and another begun, Size disappeared from the lip of the grave to speak for a while on his huge mobile phone, and returned minutes later in a state of irritation, hitching his trousers and combing his hair with the tips of his Camel-stained fingers.

Back in a bit, he said. Lunchtime. Carol's too swamped to come down. He watched Clemens. Work up an appetite while I'm gone. That last one set us back some.

They gutted the plot while Size was gone, and muled the casket out the hole, and carted it across the road to lie beneath the tarp. Then rested. When the Nissan pulled up and Size got out, he appraised the men for layabouts, when even the most work-inured of the youngbloods was a shovelful short of collapse.

For the first time that week, Size sat and ate with them, propped on a vaguely ergonomic sort of cushion that he wedged beneath his ass for driving. Scarred with cigarette burns and threadbare of weave it looked like something pillaged from a city wrecking yard, and the man atop it not much better, sitting cross-legged, like a yogi on a drunk.

Trespassajeros, he said with a nod. Trespassajeros en la noche, senores. Have you seen these? He turned to Clemens. Scattered all among the graves.

He held a puzzle piece like a Rorschach shape between his thumb and forefinger.

Who do you think it could be? said Clemens.

Devil worshippers, Size said and made horns. Gather out here of a night, light fires, sacrifice their family pets.

Maybe it was thrown from a car, said Clemens.

Thrown from a car to what end? said Size. Puzzles for all! Like a promotional thing? Hell no. His smiled faded. It's a resident spook. Someone comes here when we're gone.

One of the youngbloods turned to Jesus, spoke a couple words to him in Spanish and laughed. It might or might not have been lost on the foreman, who chewed absently with his eyes on the tramp.

Maybe if we gather all the pieces, said Size, they'll spell out his name in the grass.

Returning to the graveyard along the dim roads as familiar to him as a youth unremembered, Clemens stopped at Carol's diner just outside the plate-glass window. It was a quintessential diner of that region: rectangular, long, fluorescent-lit, with a colorful mosaic, visible from the road, spanning its façade. He crossed the intersection to the opposite side where he could watch the happenings. He did not think that he was seen, and he was right, he crossed in shadow. Both car and foot traffic were sparse. The black air glittered with cold.

For a while he could only see the patrons. They lifted food into their mouths and talked across the low-slung tables, divided from the kitchen by a row of dark backs, men playing bachelor at the bar. The head of a fry-cook could be seen time to time, making down the line with something hot in his hands. Carol appeared on the scene out of nowhere. Suddenly, she was walking through. The way she bore her tray was expert. Three cups of water, two of coffee, one of milkshake, and a pair of complicated foods. She stood primly before a booth, set the orders on the table, nodded at each of the customers there, and carried the empty tray away. On her way back through the dining room she glanced at the window that fronted the street, though whether she saw herself or Clemens or the lamp-littered blur of the darkened street, he could not say with confidence. Then she disappeared.

Back in the graveyard it was night. Frozen beads of water on the trees, branches swaying, a bright and tinselly chiming sound. The air, without its night birds in it, hissed with winter cold. He came down the hill, and through the trees, and onto the flats where the graveyard began, but stopped at the edge to mark a figure sitting on a plain of dark, which gradually became Bertrand, waiting on top of a headstone. The lights of Danielle's house were few. The road adjacent clear of headlights. The little boy refused to speak until Clemens stood there in front of him.

Fancy meeting you, he said.

What do you mean? said Clemens.

Just, fancy.

When Clemens pitched his bedroll down, Bertrand startled briefly, his shoulders drawn up. Clemens slouched a little bit, hoping it would settle him.

What are you doing out here? said Clemens.

The little boy shrugged.

Not a care in the world. Did you know that your father is looking for you?

The boy shrugged again. Probably, I did know.

You still haven't answered my question, said Clemens.

You ask a lot of them, is why.

Clemens came closer. Why did you run away?

I was keen on somewhere else. He rose and walked a narrow circle. I slept in a box by the side of the road, and I slept in the woods beneath some trees, and I jumped on a train, but got kicked off, and here I am to tell you.

But you've only been gone since yesterday.

I know, said the boy. But I've seen things.

Are you going to answer my question?

Okay.

Why don't you sit down.

He sat.

Is it your dad? The way he hits you?

Sometimes he hits. Sometimes he doesn't.

What do you mean by that?

You know.

Clemens looked at him, away, and then back.

How long has that been going on?

But the answer to that seemed beyond him; he sulked.

I did see a stag, said Bertrand. Yesterday. He stood at the edge of the road, then crossed.

Clemens sat down on the grave nearest him. Quite a rack he must've had.

You're right, said Bertrand. This wide. He demonstrated. Wide enough to kill a car.

What did you do? said Clemens.

I watched.

You're brave.

Thank you. But I was scared.

Do you need to stay here tonight? said Clemens.

I was just about to ask.

Well, you can have the sleeping bag, I guess.

No way.

Yeah, said Clemens. It's yours. Go on.

Bertrand crept around to the bag and unrolled it; Clemens heard his fingers mussing.

Then a pair of headlights burned and started toward them down the hill. Bertrand turned around at the flash of their coming and his small head was framed in the glare of them, briefly. By how they juddered down the hill, Clemens could tell they belonged to a truck.

Here comes your dad.

Hide me, said the boy.

Clemens hesitated.

Please, hide me, said Bertrand.

For starters, get behind that grave.

Clemens turned into the oncoming headlights.

Go up the hill and cross the road and find somewhere good at the edge of the trees. The minute your dad is gone for good, I'll come up there and let you know.

This is really something, Mister Clemens.

Okay.

I'll repay the favor soon.

Shut your mouth for now, said Clemens. When the truck's headlights turn off, you run.

The pickup truck slewed to a stop in the grass. Sheets of winter dust went arcing. Clemens heard Bertrand making hard for the road, and then the pickup's creaking door. Size lumbered down among the graves, motored along by the steam of his breathing.

Where's my boy? I saw him here. Not a minute ago, I saw the two of you talking.

I don't know what you mean, said Clemens. You were the last one to see him, not me.

He stood before Clemens, a pale amorphism, in nothing but jeans and a white undershirt.

I've seen the way you look at him. I know a degenerate when I see one. And I know when a man gets to hating himself for feelings that he can't control.

Like I told you, he's not here.

I'm guessing that's your final answer?

Clemens gave the briefest nod.

So then you know what's coming next?

I'm pretty sure I do, said Clemens.

I'm going to hit you in the face. Did you hear that Bertrand? Bertrand! This man is going to take a fall unless you show yourself, you hear?

Not sure who you think's going to answer, said Clemens. Like I told you, he's not here.

Size grabbed his shoulder and swung at his head. The blow caught him under the eye, on the cheekbone, and the darkness went strobic with pain on that side. Clemens stumbled into the headstone behind him, flipped over backward on top of a placard and lay gasping there in the dirt. Size came on.

He's my son, said Size. Not yours. You were only passing through. You can hit me all you want. You're not going to hear me say it.

The hell I'm not, said Size. Get up.

When Clemens did not, Size bent to assist him, dragging him up by his collar.

Why don't you fight back? he said. What in the hell are you trying to prove?

His breath was sweet with peppermint, a taint of cigarettes beneath it. He drove Clemens forth across the graves with his toes just dragging on the ground, but stopped arbitrarily, or so it seemed to Clemens, somewhere towards the middle of the yard.

I've never liked you. Since the first time I saw you. You've got an attitude to the power of ten. You think you know us all so well—us poor working stiffs out here in the county. But you don't know the half of us, and what you think you know is wrong. He began to shake Clemens. Where's my boy?

Clemens did a muffled grunt. He shook his head as best he could, and spit some blood on Size's shoe. He was actually not looking at Size at all, but straining to see behind him.

And then he was falling through the night with the cold air rushing around his bulk until Size and the moon behind him tipped and the vast crinkling sea of the tarp bore him low. It had been almost a ten-foot fall and not much softened by the tarp. But he could still move all his limbs. He heard the sound of labored breathing. He shifted his head and he scanned his surroundings. He could feel the loose dirt sifting out of his hair. The grave had a new, complicated horizon with the tarp caved in amidst the hole, with ruffles and frills along the edges and folds of tarp surrounding Clemens, so that he had the sensation, looking up, of lying at the center of a giant gift-basket, with Size's crumpled silhouette perched there on the rim like a figurine. For Clemens noticed everything; he could not afford not to notice one detail; and this, in good part, is what made Clemens Clemens, who now lay very still and waited. There was the sound the tarp made, as of a heavy, constant rain, as the last of it settled in place around Clemens. There was the rattle of dirt down into the hole and along the voluminous folds of plastic to reach a common end against him, shoring in his limbs. There was the shabby indistinctness of Size saying something and starting to slide down the side of the hole, and in his place, there was Bertrand, watching palely from above, about to say something himself, or maybe nothing, torn between the two, it seemed. Clemens urged the boy with all his being not to speak. Size grew larger, darker, meaner, tripping and stumbling down the grade. And still Clemens lay there, in pain but at peace, open to the wide, dark sky, and happy to begin his life on such outstanding terms.

Them Bones

We'd been biking along the Western tracks—we being me and my pal C.J.—when we found what was left of the old-timey soldier packed in a gulley to the east of the ties. Walking our rides for the last mile or so, we'd been scouring the ground for dislodged spikes—I had a solid eight or nine in my pack, and C.J. four, which irked him some. It was C.J., however, who'd come on the soldier, sort of hid out in the shade of the bank, like he'd stopped for a while to rest his bones or tend to a snake-bite or stake out an ambush, and just gave up the ghost right there, damned if he'd go any farther. There wasn't much of him to speak of apart from a little nest of bones, what we counted as thirteen round brass buttons, and an oval piece of something, also brass by the look of it, with the big letter C and half of an S etched cross-wise into the face before it up and faded into nothing at the edge. C.J. was pretty frothed up about that—the letters on the faded belt-buckle, I mean. Sure as we were standing there, those letters meant he'd been a Someone.

He could be a founding father. Or maybe a Spanish explorer, said C.J.

He's pretty much dust, I said, squinting at him. If he were either of those, he would be even less.

Seeing you're some kind of expert, said C.J., bring him home and show your dad.

Leander's the expert, I said. Not me. I don't even see a skull.

So what? said C.J. Bones are bones. They're bound to be worth something to somebody.

But I've got nine whole spikes in here.

Then you won't even notice the extra, he said. It was a twist to his lips and a shade to his eyes that in so many words said, Lose your pussy, and it made a body wonder why you bothered in the first place, knowing that look was in his camp. He was a raw and boxy boy and tall, with close-cut hair, a fierce, short nose and dimples that were murder on the ladies.

All right? he said.

I nodded at him.

All right, then. He clapped his hands.

Most of the bones in the shelf were thin and hollow as a finger-trap. No one among them proved much longer than my forearm or C.J.'s calf, he being some inches taller than me, which made the longest bone pretty long, all considered. If they came from when I thought they did—which C.J. was set on my step-dad confirming—then to be as intact as we had found them was a miracle of earth and weather. What with the Western bearing down and eroding the bank for a hundred years plus, and the snow that we got in Hagerstown, which always fell thicker just across the state-border, and the searching and the probing of the hobos and the drunks and the murderers, probably, along these ties, and now I thought it, boys like us, as bored and nosy as we were, the remains of the soldier looked a sight better, even, than what you might call worse for wear. The faded belt-buckle was shocking to hold, the weight of a small-gauge firearm, maybe, and the featureless half of it worn so smooth that I could see my cheek and a part of my eye deformed in the warp of the brass.

When I had squared the bones away and cinched my pack a little tighter, C.J. rifled in his own and handed me a Swisher-Sweet. The flavor was grape, but I took it from him and angled it between my teeth. C.J. tandem lit our cigars with his Zippo and eased down onto the side of the tracks.

We'll smoke these for him, he said. Our soldier. May he bring us change for beer.

I looked at C.J. and I smiled. Amen. I felt a few doubts slip away. Bless his soul.

Since we were technically in Pennsylvania, some thirty miles north of Hagerstown, we decided to follow the tracks back home instead of the highway we'd rode in on. Both of us rode chopper Schwinns, with a long shifting gear and a cranked-up seat; C.J.'s was red and mine dark blue, though I probably would've called it gunmetal, if you asked me. Shantytowns of trackside living. A granny in the half-light, drinking something on her porch. Rusted tombs of disused freight-cars, rusted auto-bodies in between, rusted barrels. The rich, rusted light of a Chesapeake sunset with C.J. stamped against it, peddling. Oncoming cars, headlights fencing through the trees, the sound of them passing abridged, now and then, by the roaring abyss of a truck or a bus. And when night had fallen, through the gaps in the trees, which complicated as we rode, the plum apparition of a fox or stray dog chasing parallel to our wheels.

When we rode across the city-limit, it was pretty close to nine o'clock, a fact that was plain in the sight of the waiters in the last open places on Potomac Street putting up tables and mopping down floors in the wake of the dinnertime rush. Men were out smoking in front of the bars and women, so few, sidling in past their hoots— men who had worked for the traitorous Fairchild before it up and moved to Texas, and a lot of whom had gotten jobs as sign painters or baggage handlers or engine technicians up at Hagerstown-Regional. But it was never the same, any of them would have told you, because working for the airlines was a customer business and none of them much good at sales. They were men who we guessed were a lot like our fathers had either of them stuck around, but they hadn't, and the messiness of it, not having a father, was rubber cement between C.J. and I—though I sort of had one, or in theory I did, this big, awkward guy named Leander DeMills. Most of the time he was only the guy who my mother had married before she kicked off, and he lived in my house, sure enough, and he sonned me, but was nevertheless, through and through, just a step. C.J.'s old man had been got by lung cancer when he was fearsome young, like five, but he still had a mother, and an older brother, Handsome, who were both pretty much in a working condition, even if Handsome was an asshole sometimes, and even if Maxie, C.J.'s mom, worked double-shifts at an Applebee's in Howard, and came home late with winey eyes. My mom had been killed in a drunk-driving crash. She was the one who was drunk, and she died. But the car that she hit had a family inside, and they had survived to her credit. I lived with Leander in a concrete split-level that backed up onto warehouse row. My own dad had left just before I was born, which made it pretty hard to hate him. He couldn't have known, wherever he was, that he was missing out on me, as opposed to a bump in his sweetheart's shirt that kept him from getting things done how he liked them.

At the corner where we parted ways—C.J. to the west and me to the north—C.J. braked his bike and turned. He was sweaty and gaunt in the fall of the streetlights.

Be in touch about those bones.

And then he rode off through the dark.

It was summer or bust in the old neighborhood. Stoops were alive all down my block. That was the thing about nine in late June in the rowhouse district where I lived: the lying and the swearing and the munching on ribs between Newports and Natty Bo's went on right where you could see it, each address a new establishment. It was mostly the sixteen to twenty-five set who stayed out yelling past politeness, and more often than not churned up in a brawl that became legendary for the forty-eight hours before a greater one commenced. So if Trey, for example, got curbed on a Tuesday and had to get his jaw wired shut, then by Thursday, Trey's boys, if they had any sap, would have to beat down the four guys who had done it. And so the birdie stayed in play until someone died or a general truce or the cops patrolled the block too often, basically screwing up everyone's fun, reminding us all where it was that we lived. It was a frightening lesson about growing up poor: no one likes to be reminded. C.J.'s brother Handsome was of that age, and certainly that disposition, but him and his crew of five or six tended to dwell on the borders of things, like a special forces unit too good for the riff-raff. All of them wore those white skirt-shirts that come in packs of six or twelve, and they walked down the street in a way that meant business, but the sort that you didn't want to know what it was; and that's the way I always saw them, a serious cadre of dudes, ranked abreast, taking their ease through a part of the world where they were high up on the food-chain. In the morning in the gutters there were huge casseroles of stripped corncobs and naked ribs and empty Utz bags and cigarette butts, and to get the right side of your brain fired up, a wet, exhausted gloss of condoms.

Where I lived was weirdly quiet compared to the bedlam three doors down, probably on account of the row of abandoneds that cut my house off from the rest of the block. The unit's ground-floor lights were on. I locked my Schwinn around the side. We had moved to this place from a much nicer one the year after mom went and wrecked up her Datsun, a plain rowhouse down C.J.'s block with a couple giant oaks for company. This had all come, the move, I mean, when Leander had lost near to half of his arm at the box factory where he'd worked for ten years. He'd landed a pretty decent sum when the maiming was ruled not his fault in the courts, but according to him not nearly enough to carry us more than a year and a half, and that was if we really stretched it. Which was a nice way of saying not nearly enough for Leander to sit on his ass for a while and focus on the classes he'd been dying to take at Howard Community College in Savage. He'd never gotten more than a high school degree, yet had, as he called them, inquisitive callings, and a couple stray credits in Civil War History, which was Leander's pet interest, were supposed to bridge the gap, I guess, between what was and might have been.

He was staked out on the couch today, hunkered over his books like a carrion kite, and when I eased in through the door he shot me bright, distracted eyes and started nodding crazily, but then without speaking went back to his book, tracing a line of the text with his finger, sort of half-sitting, half out of his seat. He traced the words with his good hand, the freak one hanging out of sight. He may've even had it jammed in between the cushions of the couch where he sat, or piled with the itchy and purposeless pillows that lined the velour from end to end, because a bunch of them tumbled off the edge in a spaz episode as I crossed to the kitchen and the next thing I saw he was plowing them up in great wobbling armfuls from off of the carpet.

What's the score, big Bren? he said. Break any records today on that thing?

Nah, I said. Just riding round.

You and C.J.? he said.

I nodded. Who else?

There could be someone else, he said.

But in truth, I knew, there couldn't be, and that was the thing about Leander: he was forever getting after the obvious stuff, pretending it was some big mystery, when, needless to say, it wasn't most times, and the habit ran afoul of my nerves.

He navigated off the couch with his freak arm and ponytail both in full swing, the former different colors either side of his elbow—haler-looking at the bicep where the flesh had been spared, but uncanny and stiff from the forearm on down, like a mannequin's arm, busted out of a store, had been grafted on what was left of a real one. The ponytail fell to midway down his back and was an altogether foolish affair in my book, but it was Leander's pride and glory and he tended it relentlessly, washing it with horse's shampoo, Mane 'n Tail, and brushing it hundreds of times a day like some sort of fairytale princess.

Powerful busy, he said. Finals week. Antietam strategics of Lee and McClellan. When you look at diagrams of the battle—some mess. Lee was just feeding his boys to the fire like they were self-replenishing.

Isn't that something, I said.

Leander frowned. It was something to those that were killed, I suppose. Bloodiest battle in the war. Twenty-three-thousand dead and wounded. More of us died on that day in September between the hours of five and five than any one since on American soil. My, big Bren, it was a doozy. Rivers of blood to the sea, down in Sharpsburg.

That's a lot of rotten luck.

Tell that to the guys who bore it. They were scattered for miles—over fields, dumped in wells, left there to rot where they lay. Like meat.

I thought to tell him about the bones, but it would take some working up to; there was something propulsive in him then that I was scared of setting loose.

Are you going to be here much longer? I said. I was going to watch some tube.

He looked a little disappointed when I said that, and he shrugged. I could pack it up to my room, if you want, but you can watch tube and me study at once.

I don't want to bother you, I said.

Not at all.

Finals, I said. They count for a lot.

But I wanted to be by myself, and he sensed it and looked pretty crushed to know the truth, and besides, had I said to myself, Aw, hell, why not let him sit and read, he would've gabbed about his battles right through the bulk of the Sunday night roster, and there was nothing on earth that I liked better after sixty plus miles of riding rough than a couple senseless hours of tube without Leander on the scene. But then he got this look to him, a sort of hazing over and retreating inward, that for all the times that I had seen it never failed to bring me low. First of all because it meant that Leander felt bad in a powerful way that I was more or less to blame for, and second of all because it put me in mind of a side of Leander that I'd seen less and less in the two years since my mother's death, whereas before that it was pretty much constant. Like the two state cops who'd brought the news—Tweedledum and Tweedledee, as Leander and me had come to call them—were standing outside our door again with their clipboards and their mannered eyes, asking if we knew the lady who drove the '82 Datsun 240Z that had been found on the side of US Route 11 diminished by half its original size. In the first couple months after we got the news, and after the funeral, which we'd had to do cheap, Leander had gotten that same look about him at least five times throughout the day. I'd had to bring him out of it with snaps or claps or by shouting his name; but no matter how I managed it, he'd always be poised to leave again, like, for instance, while washing a dish, which he'd drop, and stare at the shards piled onto his shoes, or in the middle of telling me any old thing, like a joke or a chore I'd forgotten to do, Leander would flee from the seen and sensed world to somewhere that I wasn't welcome, and it would just be me, alone, with him trembling at the borders.

I was willing to bet he had been in that place on the day that he had lost his arm, even though the maiming had been ruled a malfunction of the paper reel that he was loading. The arm was mangled flat as toast. The docs had to scrap it clear up to the elbow, and fit him a fake one that he could afford—and though I don't think that I had all the details, or the logic they'd been forged amidst, I figured Leander had taken the cheapie to maximize the part of the claim he could use to help us get back on our feet money-wise.

Which is a hell of a thing, when you really think on it. Though I managed not to, a good part of the time.

My mom, who'd been a party-girl—a smoker of Pall Mall cigarettes, an admirer of choppers and full-sleeve tattoos, a watcher of dawn through the plate-glass of bars and the portals of drunk-tanks a couple of times—had probably met him on a night when the world had seemed too vast and cruel for her to navigate by herself any longer. I think of her listing on top of her stool, and Leander, next to her, taking her by the wrist so that she rebounded right into his arms. And I think of the strength of his box-maker's fingers—maybe even the ones of the hand that he'd lose—becoming the only unshakeable thing in the headachy slur that was her world, and persisting to be until she left it, and me behind, at thirty six.

Leander was still in nowheresville, staring at me, but also past me, tapping the thigh of his stonewash jeans with the five working fingers that he had to his name; he was lost, I imagined, to the long, skinny hall with the halogen light constantly on the blink that Leander's mind sometimes became when all life's answers had escaped him.

I'd better be getting upstairs, he said. You also pay rent, in a manner of speaking.

Come on, Leander. You know that I don't.

I wish you wouldn't call me that.

Dad, I said, but so, so quiet that neither of us could really hear. Can't a guy sit by himself and relax without five hundred words on why?

Sure, he said. I just get touchy. I think you're a pretty cool guy, is the reason. Hey—how's this? He clapped his hands, like I was the one who was starved for his company, which sounded unnatural— the clap, I mean, on account of the dry and muted pitch of the mannequin's hand on the genuine one—and I thought of a whole stadium of Leanders, clapping and cheering to herald a play, and what it would sound like multiplied, all that heartache and fear in the dry, smacking thousands. When I finally came back to the room we were in and the conversation we'd been having, he was on the subject of his finals again, how they had him pretty gagged and bound, but that when they were over, which would be, like, tomorrow, then we could spend some time together, which wasn't to say that I should feel pressure, because that was no fun, and fun we'd be having; rather we should focus on a fun circumstance amenable to both of us, like a slasher flick, maybe, or an all-ages mosh—did I happen to know that this man, of all people, liked the scorched earth assault of a drop-D guitar?

Maybe not tomorrow, he said, but Tuesday. And if then is no good, the day after that.

You mean Wednesday, I said, to give him grief.

That's the one, he said, all nods.

And here was one thing that Leander had taught me: kindness can be a kind of toughness. It can make you as close to unfuckwithable as any tough guy is likely to get.

Wednesday then? I said, and got up, and crossed to the couch, where I sat.

He kept nodding.

Leander, I said.

He wore a half-witted grin.

Earth to Leander DeMills, I said.

Huh, he said. Then smiled. Aw, hell. I got to go see about these flashcards.

And like we hadn't talked at all, he wandered up the stairs.

On the next day, which was Monday, I slept in till late, and watched the tube till even later: the last of the rerun cartoons on the networks, badly drawn and worsely dubbed, followed by the odd-couple sitcoms, also reruns, yet weirder somehow than the color cartoons, and finally the talk-shows, all tragic and loud, with their nasty surprises offstage in the greenroom, while the infomercials jostled one another in between to get me to apply for an interest-free loan, or enroll in a trade or business college, or set what looked to me like a landmine on wheels on a cleaning rampage throughout my house, until at last I didn't know who I was anymore, there was so much to do, or at least, be attempted, and I yanked up the shades, and I cranked the AC, and wondered why I felt so low.

Leander was out laying hurt on his finals.

C.J. came by around 2 p.m.

Instead of knocking on the door or giving the doorbell a buzz like a pal, he shouted to me from the street, on his bike, without his kickstand even levered, like he'd happened to stop there in front my house and thought he'd raise me while he was. I sort of canted through the door in nothing but a pair of boxers, sipping a Diet Dr. Pepper that Leander bought in packs of twelve.

Grab your wheels and come down here. Handsome wants to talk to you.

To me, I said. What for? I'm nude.

You look half-dressed to me, said C.J.

I looked around the neighborhood for any sign of anyone, but there was only summer calm and the sound of a hose dousing weeds up the block.

What for? I said. I'm on sabbatical.

Sabba—what the hell? said C.J. He scanned the scene, too. It's concerning those bones.

I thought you wanted me to show them to Leander.

Is he around?

I shook my head.

So you *haven't* shown him?

Again, with the headshake. But C.J., he seemed pretty set.

Do you need me to help you put your pants on?

He stirred up the air with one hand in impatience and kicked his pedals pointlessly, everything about him awhir at that moment and shit-pantsed as a UM pledge, which, I'll admit, in the five years I'd known him, was a way I'd never seen him look.

We rode our bikes not to Handsome's place, because Handsome still lived with his mom and with C.J., but rather to a guy named Bo's, who lived a little uptown from the summertime circus in a studio apartment nestled in among others, the paint having dried on the whole complex no more than a year before, then hustled out cheap to whoever had bread with an imminent hike in the rent in the small-print. There was even a little gated courtyard to make you believe that you'd moved up a rung, but the tiling on the benches had a stiff, Lego texture, and the potted plants looked laminated, and the fountain bone-dry save a sludge of run-off where the residents chucked their cigarettes—in other words, it was a dump that had managed to look slightly better than one. But C.J., at least, was impressed with the place, where it seemed he'd never been before, because as soon as we buzzed at the scrap-metal gate and got the reciprocal buzz to enter, I could hear him say under his breath, Some digs, as he ran his hand over his minimal haircut.

Outside of Bo's apartment, which was on the ground floor, we waited for someone to come out and get us, while the sliding-glass door shook with music so loud that it threatened to set the pane loose from its housing.

It slid open. A guy stood there. He was chugging a tall boy of Bo to his dome, and wearing blue jeans and a black Ravens jersey that were both some outlandish exponent of Large, and his arms, so thin that you pitied him, almost, were worked with a tangle of blotchy tattoos. But when he pitched the beer away, revealing his neck, which his arm had concealed, we were both of us given our shock for the week by the sight of a giant, supple scar that spanned the guy's neck from jaw-hinge to jaw-hinge. Like he'd had his throat cut, and then made whole again, and here he was to tell us how. I'd pegged him at first for about Handsome's age, which as far as I knew must be nineteen or twenty, but with the scar and the tats and the meth-battered smile—a shooting-gallery of a smile, with brown stains—and a greyish aspect to his skin that vetted dark extremes of living, he could've been easily five years older, maybe even ten.

Hey, Peyton, said C.J.

Scar-neck watched us. Then lit a smoke and watched us still. You got that stuff you said you had?

He's got it, said C.J., and nodded my way.

He gave me the quick scan. Who all's that?

Brennan, said C.J. From down the way.

I ain't never seen him.

He's H-town local.

Maybe he is and maybe not.

I'm good, I said.

Oh is that so? We said go fetch, meant you, little captain.

Brennan's the one I found it with.

Scar-neck turned, blew ample smoke. Shorty's back with his first mate!

The room, I must say, was pretty smoky, so Peyton sort of disappeared, a couple other voices shouted back and we were in. But for a second, with the music, which was raging speed metal, and the smoke, which was halfsies tobacco and weed, I was all but deaf and blind and took my course by C.J.'s elbow, who was pal enough to let me grip it, homo though we might have seemed. At last the smoke-bank broke apart on a couch packed full with staring dudes, and a busted La-Z-Boy to the right, where Handsome sat. Down at the end of the couch, facing out, was a guy with some shorty sacked out in his lap, while her small, painted feet, fit with all kinds of toe-rings, wiggled bright in the lap of some guy down the line. This, I think, was Bo himself, who cottoned to me just as vaguely. Peyton leaned against the wall, recycling the fire in his cherry, all grins. The music was up so goddamned loud I was pretty impressed they could hear one another, but all the same, though, they were probably vegging, just watching the room drift past their noses.

Big Brennan, said Handsome. The skeleton man! Been keeping this little mongoloid out of trouble?

Unlike the rest of the guys and the girl, who were all drinking Natty or Bo from the can, he was nursing something in a bottle, maybe Yuengling, that he drank from like an afterthought, lifting his beer and lifting his beer until a bit of it happened to spill down his throat. There was more than a likeness between him and C.J., which had always sort of creeped me out, like God or whoever, having made the first brother and seen what he'd amounted to, had been trying to hide his mistake with the younger, but in all likelihood with the same faulty cogs. Handsome wore a pirate's succession of earrings that ended way up at the top of his ear, and they glinted at me in the overhead lights when he hunched through the smoke to get a better look at me.

Not a whole lot to speak of, I said bogusly. We just been surviving the heat like ya'll.

Faggot, said C.J., and knocked me one in the ribs, which I instantly forgave him for, for were I him, he me, us there, I probably would've knocked me, too.

Handsome laughed. Ease off, little captain. Aren't we surviving the heat?

The thugs grumbled.

Surviving the heat and then some, he said. Ya'll need a beer or a bong or whatever?

C.J. stepped forward. Both for me.

I'll take a Bo, I told Bo, and received one.

The beer was cooked and lacking fizz, but I drank most of it in a gulp to get centered, while C.J. trailed Bo through the fog of blunt smoke to a high, cluttered table on Handsome's right side where a dream-like contraption of rubber and glass waited for him to decipher.

When I heard what you found in Pennsylvania, I had to see it for myself. We all had to see it, he said, and they nodded. It's a once in a lifetime kind of find.

I've got it right here in my bag, I said.

Well, ain't that a fucking relief, said Peyton.

There was the gurgle and suck of the bong being cleared, and then the sound of someone hacking, followed by C.J., sidling out of the fog, which had thinned to a mist now my eyes had adjusted, a near-sighted look gathering on his face as he came around to stand beside me.

Lay him out on the carpet, Bren, my man.

So I knelt on the filthy and over-plush floor of that pre-fab room gone vague with smoke, and started to dole out the bones one by one from the unzipped mouth of my Eagle Creek backpack. C.J. sort of hovered near, making overtures to assist with his hands, suddenly kneeling, then rising again, though he was too stoned to put himself to much use. The whole group of guys, and the girl, just watched. There were six of them all told, I gleaned, unless there were others hid out in the smoke. Peyton, Handsome, Bo, the girl and two more, most of which, except the girl—who wore monogrammed jeans, and platform shoes, and a black tank-top cut away past the ribs so you just caught edge of her boob from the side—were draped in those shapeless, drugstore shirts that never seemed to spot or stain; so white, I imagined, that they might've been robes for some broke-ass, hard-drinking ordination of monks. I could hear cigarettes being lit while I worked, another bong-hit, a fresh beer getting cracked. Then I realized in my momentary panic that I'd mustered what little I knew of anatomy toward arranging the bones as they'd lived in the flesh, and was trying to recreate our soldier like Charles Motherfucking Darwin in that room full of thugs. I'd taken out the soldier's buckle to place it between what was left of the hips when Handsome called out: Bren, my man. I ditched Bio One for a reason. Quit that.

Yeah, quit that, said C.J. absurdly, before breaking down into Tommy gun laughter.

I shot him a look, like, *Thanks a lot*, which staggered the laughter a little, I guess, but the force of the weed kept him going a while and I was like to blush my death.

Can you believe these fucking guys? Peyton was shaking his head in bemusement. Handsome, remind me—and be honest now—were we this stupid at their age?

I do believe we were, said Handsome.

Them bones are disgusting, said the girl.

Them bones are sacred artifacts. We're going to pitch in to acquire them.

Well, count me out. And count out Sherman. She cradled the face of the guy she was with—a skinny, bald-headed, not bad-looking guy with a telltale spot of Negro blood—and he gazed back and forth between Handsome and her like one of them had to be selling him short. Sherman and me got plans, she said. And to broker them plans we need money, Sherm-baby. And to have us some money, we need not to be giving to the Voodoo Foundation of Maryland, hear?

Shut that black bitch up, said Peyton. I swear to Christ, Handsome, she talks blacker than Sherman.

You heard him, said Handsome, and eyed the mulatto, who brought a finger to his lips, and I wondered, was it always this way with poor Sherman, having to suffer talk like that, when all he probably wanted was a couple of pals to blaze and shoot the shit among.

By then I had laid out the last of the bones, as well as the buckle and thirteen buttons, and our soldier looked as good as he was ever going to look.

Handsome got up and strolled around and came to stand behind yours truly. The girl with the side-boob untangled from Sherman and sat sullenly on the floor.

Ain't he a beaut, said Handsome. Umm-hmm. He once was lost but now he's found. Peyton, come here for a minute, my brother. Peyton smirked and came and stood. See that C and that S on the buckle?

I see half of something that looks like an S.

You know what that stands for?

I believe that I do.

Ya'll know what that stands for? Say it proud, now.

Confederate soldier, said Bo from the table, drilling sidewise with the bong.

Careful with that thing, said Handsome. Confederate States of America, son. Skeleton Jim here gave his life that we might honor him today.

And how are you going to do that? said the girl, lighting a smoke in a pissed-off way.

Like I said, you nigger bitch. By pitching in to buy him.

Careful about that word, said Peyton. She's a nigger *loving* bitch is what she is.

Little captain, big Bren, come stroll for a minute. He motioned us to follow him. There's something I want to show ya'll.

I was reluctant, somehow, to get up from the carpet and leave our soldier lying there, but Handsome told me, He'll be fine, and C.J.

nodded at me in a fatherly way that made me want to break down laughing; but I didn't break down laughing, and I got another beer, and I followed the brothers into the next room, where the three of us stopped at a glass-fronted cabinet that Handsome opened with a key.

This is our cabinet of wonders, he said. We keep it at Bo's because Bo's is secure. Every thing behind these doors has got a soul, and a story, and a reason for being.

And he proceeded to give us the scoop on each one until my head was fairly spinning. God knows it might've been the weed, or beer number two, which I drank to beat one, but when he was done—and he really went on, giving places, and people, and dates, and connections—I felt dumber for having heard.

A Nazi officer's coat from WWII; a weasely picture of the Fuhrer; a table-lamp from 1930 whose base was a black guy in tan overalls grinning around a watermelon; a rusted-out chain once used in a lynching; statues of Mammys and Sambos and Toms; a Confederate flag folded up in the way that American flags got the treatment at camp, and in alongside it a red Nazi flag with a single black branch of the Swastika symbol aligned parallel to the crease in the fabric; a monogrammed plate with Russian letters beneath a picture of a devil with the old Jewish scrolls; collector's coins arranged by size and embossed with the portraits of various dudes: Lee and Polk and Hood and Stuart; Goebbels and Mengels and Adolf himself; a small, blackened something at the bottom of a jam-jar that you might've avoided on the street, but was—or so the seller said—the pirated scalp of a Yahi brave.

I always respect finder's rights, said Handsome. Everything here got acquired for a price. Which is why I'm proposing to you two boys to take that soldier off your hands for two hundred even, one hundred a share. But that comes with a little work, and here's the kind I mean. He addressed me: Your stepdad is keen to this stuff, I hear. I need him to give me the unrefined stats. Like for instance is he real, this guy? Was he just Yankee bait or an officer-type? Around when did he live? Around how did he die? What was the battle and who were the warriors?

I'll find out as much as I can, I said.

But everything felt strange right then.

I finished my beer.

Handsome locked up the cabinet.

C.J. looked slow to process what had happened. So are you, like, in the K.K.K.?

Nah. Handsome smiled. The hoods aren't for us. But we know guys that are, he said.

So this is all for show, said C.J. Ya'll are, like, collectors, or scientists, or something.

Sort of, said Handsome. We're proud white men. Except Sherman, that is, but he's trying damn hard.

That night, with Leander decompressing from his finals with a mayonnaise sandwich on the living room couch, I took the bones out of my bag and laid them on the coffee table. But even as I did and got shut of the guilt that was eating at me for not telling him sooner, a new kind of guilt was beginning to spread now that I'd told him at just the right time. But he didn't suspect a thing, Leander, and sat there dumbstruck for a moment, a carnage of bread and mayonnaise stuck to the top of his half-open mouth.

Where did you say that the two of you found him?

Between Hanover and Gettysburg.

Well, there you go right there, he said. Eighteen-sixty-three, three days. Meade versus Lee. The great turnaround. He might be the last unburied. This belt-buckle here. He fingered it closely. It means he was a good old boy. And these buttons, thirteen of them, all in a row—he barfed a few crumbs—they mean this fellow was an officer.

Do you think you could say what kind? I said.

Well, generals are out, he said. But he could be a captain or a colonel or a major or any number of lieutenants. Without his marching wool, who knows?

You can study at him a while, if you want.

That'd be great. Real great, Big Bren.

I'm tired, I said. I'm for the tube.

I'll go on up to my room, said Leander.

That's all right, I said. Stay on.

I would, but I'm needing my books, he said.

All right, I said. So go on up.

He paused for a minute, staring down at the soldier, and shook his head in wonderment. Touched by the hard hand of war, he said. I suppose it's up to us to deliver him home.

I steadied my voice. Can you say how he died?

Just pick a way and it might've been his. The theatre was a scary place. Shelling, and flames, and musket balls whizzing, and sabers sticking at you from the tops of hot guns. If he didn't lose his head to a cannonball or something, then a hog might've carried it off post-mortem.

That's grisly, I said.

That's life in the corps.

How did your finals come off? I asked him.

Leander did a shrug. I was tolerable ready. But when the clock started ticking, I forgot what I learned. We could go there if you want, said Leander.

Go where? I said.

To Gettysburg. To see the reenactment in July. It's a blitzer.

Ask me in July, I said.

And then I turned on the TV.

I didn't see Leander until the next day when the doorbell spoke up around ten in the morning and I plodded downstairs from the heat of my room to find Handsome and Peyton loitering on the stoop. Both of them were acting curious, like we hadn't just met the day before, especially Handsome, who couldn't stand still and kept rubbernecking past my eyes into the living room. Parked at the curb near Leander's Deville was cherry-red Toyota with a spoiler and rims.

Is your old man around? said Handsome.

I'm guessing that he's still asleep. Raise him to the task, said Peyton. We're here to get things settled up.

What all settled up? said Leander, behind me.

He was standing at the bottom of the stairs in his bathrobe.

Handsome stepped inside the house, while Peyton stood behind him looking sketchy and mean.

Hey, Mister Brennan, said Handsome. How do? I'm Handsome Folsom, C.J.'s brother, Brennan's friend.

Leander walked up rearranging his robe, and looked from Handsome to Peyton to me. He hadn't been to bed all night— you could tell from the pale concave of his face—but there was brightness in his eyes that gave a body pause to wonder. I saw that his fingers were covered in ink, which he'd smeared in broad streaks across the mint-green of his bathrobe.

Leander DeMills is my name, he said. Brennan right here is my stepson.

I told him: They're here about the soldier.

The soldier, he said. What in sam hill about?

Have you not told him yet? said Handsome.

Told me what? said Leander. Big Bren?

Handsome and Peyton want to buy him. They wanted me to give him to you to make sure.

Leander DeMills came forward laughing. Confirmed, then, boys. He's Confederate dead. Log your report with the Christian Commission.

We'll take him on his way, said Handsome.

Just wait a sec, now. Has money changed hands? Brennan, are these guys for real?

I told them yes, I said, and shrugged.

But this tired soul belongs to history. We're the only folks that he's got to speak for him. So unless ya'll are Uncle Sam, I'm going to have to keep him here.

Come on, now. Big Bren? said Handsome.

I don't know, I said. He's yours.

Then Handsome said, This is going nowhere. Let's rewind the conversation. Brennan and C.J. found him—fine. C.J. told me, and I asked to see Brennan. Brennan recommended yourself, Mr. Mills, as someone who would know the score. You say he's Secesh, but no we can't take him. To my mind, that's a pretty pickle.

I beg your pardon, son, said Leander. But what in dominion is that supposed to mean?

It means that there's been double-dealing. I just want what's owed to me.

Now, boys, said Leander, coming forward, palms up. I haven't a doubt you've got your reasons. But you can't just go barging into other folks' homes, pillaging national treasures, and such. There's got to be order. There's got to be rules. There's got to be history, or what have we come to?

You're going to be history yourself, said Peyton, if you don't—

—let's talk sense, said Handsome. I'm sure we can work something out, Mr. Mills.

Things have worked out fine by me. It's you two boys that seem put out.

Peyton pitched his smoke away and took Handsome hard by the arm from behind.

Handsome's left arm was crooked up on his hip where he appeared to be massaging the bone in vexation, but then I wondered, what's he up to? What's he got beneath his shirt?

All right, then. Some other time. We're all a little hot, I guess. He started to back down the stairs, smiling at us. We apologize to ya'll—Mr. Mills—for the trouble.

Leander said pleasantly, It's *De*-mills. And sorry about the mix-up, boys, I'm glad that ya'll take an interest in history. Would that I had from an earlier age. Stay the course, is what I say, get yourself enrolled in a good master's program, and hell, who knows, in two years' time, you could be writing that soldier's biography.

But by then the Toyota was speeding away with Peyton and Handsome arguing at the wheel, and Leander was waving, then smiling at me, and then waving again, like I should wave with him. When the car was long gone, he let out a breath and looking at me said:

Strange stuff.

Well, I am going to hear it now, I'd meant to say under my breath.

From who? said Leander. Those two guys? Hell, those two guys are green as grass. If they can't see what they owe history, what have they got to say to you? You tell them I forced the issue. Tell them that I wouldn't budge.

Okay, I said, and looked up at Leander, who was squinting his eyes in the mid-morning light. He put a hair-tie in his teeth, gathered his hair in a loose ponytail and worked the hair-tie twice around with a deftness that recalled kung-fu. And when he looked at me it was without calculation, with zero intention that I should be grateful, and probably because of this, I found out that I was.

Later, we took our Wednesday outing, which wasn't half bad as I thought it would be. We went and saw a movie at the plex you couldn't bike to. Leander parked his car as far away as he could manage in order to stroll through the mall, see the sights. Kids my age were in the stores and sitting around the tacky fountains and climbing against the escalators, pushing folks aside. Leander got a large popcorn and dusted it with Raisonettes and held it on his left pantleg where we could both get at it. The movie was about some dude who's supposed to be trained in the deadly arts, but the dude can't remember how or why on account of the fact he woke up in a bathtub, so the guy just sort of drifts along, trying to figure where he comes from, until half-an-hour in you discover that someone sowed a bomb in his chest while he laid there on ice, and it's going to go off in an hour and change, which is more or less, also, what's left of the movie, and anyway, bomb-chest survives and revenges himself on the guys who betrayed him and kills one of them with a tire-iron, I think, by shoving it into his brain through his nose. Leander liked the movie even more than I did and he gave me a list of his favorite scenes whose order he kept changing. Then we went out to a Mexican joint with a weird, rainforest décor inside, which Leander was quick to point out, at the table, was a cry from the country itself, and inaccurate. Then he reached up to the fake waterfall surmounted between the banks of tables, picked a fake lizard from among the fake rocks, dried it with his napkin and replaced it. He ordered a big tortilla soup while I sat there and munched the chips. He fouled his elbow in the soup on account of the fact it drags sometimes and overturned the steaming bowl all over the lap of his high-waisted jeans. The waitress brought another soup, but on the check it said, Bad elbow, and both me and him had a laugh about that, though I could tell that he felt dopey. All through the meal he kept mentioning the soldier, and how he would make him his project that summer.

I want to get a read on his culture, he said. To know what it would've been like to be him. Then maybe I'll write something, send it to a journal.

He never asked once about the agreement in which I'd been meaning to make him a pawn. Maybe he figured it was none of his business, or maybe he didn't want to know. He looked at me when I spoke to him, looked at me right in the eyes, and kept looking, so that sometimes I had to turn away and gaze among the plastic ferns. Other times, though, he looked away, especially toward the dinner's end, and I'd rapidly start to grow accustomed to the scared, spaced-out way I was used to him looking.

In the car driving home he said, Hell, Brennan. Let's keep on not being strangers, all right?

I looked at him and sort of smiled, but didn't wager yes or no.

All right, he said, as if I'd answered.

It seemed like a pretty good start.

A couple years before Leander, when it was just my mom and me, my mom came home a little tossed and honked the horn so I'd come out and we drove to this nickel arcade out in Frederic that was open through the smaller hours. There was hardly anybody there, and we had the run of the place, her and me. There was ski-ball and pinball and mallet-the-toad; there was punch-out, air-hockey, Pac-Man, Rampage, and those first-person games where you mow down the zombies. Walking along the banks of games with tokens clashing in our pockets, she'd lightly take my arm, my mom, and let me choose the next event. She smelled like smoke and booze and leather, with a dream of perfume, of smelling good, buried somewhere beneath the others. We spent a good two hours in there, and twenty-five dollars in change, I'll bet. On the ski-ball machine my mom got bold or maybe she'd had a few more than I thought, because she started to scramble up the ramp and drop the wood balls straight into the hundred to maximize the ticket-spew. But because we were two of just five or so gamers, and making noise to beat the games, the night-clerk of the place caught wind and came over to kick us out. There was this small, straggled girl just a couple lanes down who was there with her older kid brother, I think, and this time my mom took me hard by the arm, in a way that I knew I should follow her lead, and we dumped the lot on her, this vagabond girl—a giant, unwinding, pink labyrinth of tickets. And it had made me feel good, looking back through that door, with my mom in the lead and the night-clerk behind us, just seeing that girl, ankle-deep in our tickets, blissed out of her mind at such luck.

That week was a long, slow retreat for Leander, and one he gave his all against, but even when we were alone I could still feel the pull of the bones working on him. He could never seem to puzzle them enough or too much, like his very life was riding on it, like the bones were a sickness he thought he might have that he needed to get all the facts on. But there was dinner at first, or his best attempts at it, meals you would've had to really try to screw up: grilled cheese with bologna and tomato inside; macaroni and cheese from the box, plus Adobo; strip-steaks seasoned to a fuzz and cooked in five ounces of vegetable oil with a mess of canned beets still steeped in their gore to usher in the nutrients. Afterwards we would walk to the gas station store for a treat of chocolate or ice cream and then, while we ate, back again to the house at a slower pace always than on our way there. Then we'd sack out on the living room couch with a legion of box-fans pointed towards us and decide on a show or a movie to watch until the fog of sleep crept in. But even in those first few nights I could tell he wasn't sleepy, because as soon as I started to fade he'd get up, and switch off the tube, and herd me to bed, only to return to the couch for the night; and there I'd find him in the morning, crusty-mouthed in all his clothes, whole sections of the Hagerstown Community Library strewn across the coffee table, and often a bone, or several bones, to mark a chosen page therein. Sometimes he hadn't slept at all; I could tell from his manic good cheer when I woke. And once he tried his hand at breakfast—a meal dear to him he called egg-in-a-bread—if only to watch me pick it over, his eyes drifting couchward again and again. He kept the bones in three shoeboxes filed beneath the coffee table. They were labeled in accordance with an old diagram he'd stumbled across in Grey's Anatomy. He was Indiana Jones without the starch, without the know-how, and it wrecked my heart to watch him sleuth. He recorded lists of vanished names, any of which might be the soldier's, and a good many of them so foreign to me they might've been the names of spacemen: Asahel Nash, Orestes Brownson, Osmun Lastrobe, Orange Judd; Alvah Shuford, Charles de Spain, Lycurgus Caldwell, Phillip Slaughter. Soon the dinners stopped outright, and it was implied I should see to myself. And though the food was nothing special, I missed the ritual of the knife and the fork.

Soon correspondence began to pile up, addressed to different institutions—the Ivy League names written bold and precise across the white of stick-on labels. And now he was typing late into the night on the supercomputer he'd purchased by mail, an overstocked model all blips and green-screen that hastened to black when it got overheated, and printing off those reams of paper whose edges took a miracle of surgery to prune. These I found on every surface, and between every cushion of the couch, thick as lint.

As for the pages, they said funny things, or things that made no sense to me, or it wasn't that they made *no* sense, but that I saw no point in them, and the pointlessness of it, at last—well, it creeped me, made me wonder: Who *is* he? And I thought of that oldie-but-goodie fright flick that's set in that mammoth hotel in the mountains, when the father—thank Jesus he wasn't the stepdad—goes utterly batshit toward the end. It's a hard, freaky truth that the mother discovers only when she reads his jabber, and that moment, well, shit, there is no moment like it, when she flips through the pages and lo they're the same. Leander's pages weren't the same, but they were damn alike mutations—false starts, by the look of them, the meat of each phrase hacked away like a limb.

> History shows that the dead may be raised…
> or,
> May the dead be raised, says History….
> or,
> History, the great resurrector compels us…
> or,
> Raise up a toast that the dead may be raised…

On and on it went for pages, Leander's own little bright corner of madness. Though, truth be told, it didn't scare me so much as it made me just powerfully sad.

By the end of the week there was no more pretending. Leander was in a losing fight. He'd bought some rolls of chicken wire and a couple special sewing needles, and when I walked in he would hardly look up so tricky was the task at hand: pricking the bones at either end, threading them along the wire, bending the wire first here, now there; and at last standing back from his design to recognize the coming man when in truth there were gaps—just preposterous ones—that he would have to labor to ignore, knowing him. I rationed my time just touring round, sometimes as far as Pennsylvania, but never along that stretch of tracks where me and C.J. found the bones. And I always came home in the late afternoon when Leander was sure to be asleep to get a dose of tube in me before I went up to my room for the evening. But he would always be there at the edge of my vision, tending to his bones and wire.

When Leander had all the parts reordered, he called me downstairs from my room to admire it.

It was the first time, I think, in three whole days that I hadn't had to squawk just to get his attention.

Since he worked so close to the glass coffee table, his spectacles tended to fog up completely, and that was how I saw him when I entered the room, Buchenwald-skinny and pale as a grub, wiping the haze from his eyes with a shirt-cuff.

Check him out, Leander said. Fit enough to build a breastwork.

He looks mostly there.

Mostly there, said Leander.

Figured a name for him yet? I said.

Not yet, he said. But I'm closing on one. It's just statistics, to my thinking, deriving the mean from which names were the rage. Alvah's a probable one. He shrugged. But so is Ephraim. Edward. Henry. Whatever it is, though, it's got to sound right. It's got to choose him, you know? Names do.

What about rank?

Still up for debate.

Well, how about the scrape he died in?

Gettysburg, said Leander. That I know. On account of where you two boys found him. Like as not he wandered there, touched with a kill-shot or crazy with fever. But then again, like I said, there was a power of beasts that liked to drag these boys afield. He might well have been one of those—the unlucky.

That took you three days? I said.

Leander did a laugh. You mean only three, right?

No, I said. I don't mean that.

You mad at me, Bren? Leander's voice began to tremble. If you are, then just say so.

I'm not mad, I'm just amazed. That that took you three days to do. I mean, what are your plans, Leander—hell? You going to hang him from the porch when it turns Halloween?

Well okay, Bren, he said. Okay. I didn't know you cared one way or another.

He sat heavily on the couch and looked round like he was going to cry or something, and I wanted him to, in so many words, just to see someone, somewhere, cry. And I wanted to tell him I do care, and I wanted to tell him I am mad, and I wanted to ask him if my being mad—the kind of mad you can't deny—was the only way to make him see the sorrows he'd brought down on me.

Because how could you ask a guy like that—a guy that queer, a guy that dopey—yes, how could you ask a guy like that to please not leave you in his dust?

The red Toyota came for me a couple days later, purring along the curb at twilight, while the voices of Handsome and Peyton and Bo and C.J., I thought I could hear, underneath them, called to me to stash my bike and take a little ride. Well ain't it come down on me soon, I allowed, though I knew in my heart that it should've come sooner. But for a while there was only the grumbling motor and the ratcheting tick of me walking my bike, and I willed that they go on forever, those sounds, if it meant putting off what I had to do next.

Which was stop, so that the car stopped, too. And be all right with come what may.

He's pretending he ain't never met us, said Peyton. He was grinning at me, elbow propped on the door, a Newport burning in his fingers.

It appears that he's got shy, said Handsome. But we aren't put out, are we, C.J.?

Hell no, said C.J., sitting shotgun with Handsome, while Peyton leaned out of the shadow they made, and a figure who was likely

Bo camped out in deeper darkness still, the four of them sitting, visible, then obscured, in a sort of checker pattern organized by the streetlights.

Come and take a ride, said Handsome. We just want to get our drink on.

Where? I said.

Somewhere different. You'll see.

C.J.? I said, and he shrugged, like, *Come on,* though it didn't do much in the way of assurance, so thickly ingrown did the four of them seem, a process more than one week in and by now bearing ugly fruit.

But I had learned to read my friend better than Leander, even. Indecision squirmed in him, at the corners of his mouth and in the centers of his pupils, which signaled to me that whatever it was I was giving myself over to in that moment would never amount to the sideshows of pain that I had witnessed on these streets: a crack-rock lieutenant who'd been beaten so bad his skin was camouflage with bruises; a queer who'd been given the permanent scream when he was made to french the curb. Had Handsome had it in for me—and I mean *really* had it in—then C.J., or so I sorely hoped, would've been more than just squirmy.

Peyton got out so that I could get in and would have to ride bitch in between Bo and him, both of whom smelled six beers deep and gag-me sweet with cigarettes. A beer got deployed from somewhere in the front and reached backward into my hands. Unlike before, it was cold as creekwater and soothed my nerves a bit to taste. Everyone else held a beer in his hand or had one pressed between his knees, and the floor of the car was a graveyard of suchlike, which made your every shift an outburst.

Handsome chopped his hand at me in the empty space between the seats.

No excuses, Bren my man. We got our wires crossed is all. Sure, your old man did a thing, but you've got a lifetime to do him one better. C.J.'s retarded in most every thing. Family is as family does.

Get fucked, Handsome.

You first, little captain.

C.J. smiled and did a laugh and his eyes, real quick, met mine in the rearview. So what have you been up to, Bren?

Mostly just tooling around on the Schwinn.

Any bones out there? said Handsome.

Nary a one. I returned C.J. 's glance. But then I can't be sure without a second pair of eyes.

A beat of weird and wondrous silence. Holy shit, did I feel green. But then something gave way around me, a sort of restoration of the air in the car, like every one there had been holding his breath, me not least among them.

It was Peyton who was the first to speak, with a good-natured scoff in advance of his words: Well doesn't that beat all for cute. There was real love lost between these queers.

And then he looked ahead of him with a face that seemed suddenly different to me, not friendly, exactly, but gratified, maybe, like I had passed some test or other. He gestured me to drink my beer and when I had finished it passed me another, and handed others round the car to a lively and general swilling.

Here go, here go, here go, here go. Then pausing to eye me. And here go, too.

And with everyone smiling, including myself, and then with a little unease, but oh well, the car bucked speeding down the road and darkness closed its wings around us.

We'd been riding around in the dark for a while, just shooting the shit about the O's and adding to the rubble of domestic at our feet, when Handsome turned down an access road off the state highway we'd been driving upon that swerved, and humped, and crunched along to a maimed instance of chain-link fence.I was only middling buzzed, but buzzed enough to feel courageous because soon the car stopped and the dome-lights went on and I was getting out with the four them. Handsome and Bo walked on ahead while

Peyton lurked back by the car for a time and then started walking himself, but behind us. We had switched to a thirty of Yuengling en route, the sea-green, labeled, twist-off kind, and Handsome and Bo smashed the ones they were drinking on what sounded like a bank of concrete. C.J. looked at me and smiled and, shrugging, did the same with his. It landed in the weeds beyond, rolled around a bit and stilled.

Good to see your ass, said C.J.

Good to see your ass right back.

Ya'll walk fucking *slow*, we heard, from where the car was parked in darkness.

Peyton came toward us, eternally smoking, his shoulders and arms as white as paint.

It came to me then we were under the highway, climbing the vault that spanned under the girders, like the legs of brontosauri in the first dark of evening. The five of us clambered up the incline, hunched where the floor met the ceiling and sat. It felt at least ten degrees cooler in there. Distant lights and distant honking. The call for a blunt sounded out in the dark and Peyton handed me the works, a cherry-flavored Philly and a sifting ziplock bag. But I could hardly see my hands and rolled the thing unevenly and goobered up the smoking end while trying to smooth out the tumors. I handed the sopping blunt to Handsome, who reached me a beer for my troubles and laughed.

Am I supposed to smoke this thing, or lick it so it doesn't melt?

It sort of looks pregnant in the middle, said someone.

Maybe it's got stomach cancer.

C.J., you need to school this boy. This is pretty shameful shit.

All right, so my cheeks burned a little. I would like to see yours not.

It was Handsome who sparked the runty thing, taking quick, breathy drags before passing to Bo, and so it came around to me, gummy through the middle. My legs got disconnected from my top as we sat there, and I sipped at a beer to kill the scratch in my throat. The conversation happened through me, prisms of words and sounds and names.

Peyton's raw face leaned out of the dark. Ya'll want to know how I got it? he said. It's a story to chill your fucking blood.

He seemed to be talking about his scar, though I was unsure how we had arrived there. A weird sort of sadness came over the group like we were going to say a prayer.

I'm listening, said C.J.

Peyton turned to regard me. What about you, featherweight? he said.

I looked at him and he looked ugly, not only head-on but through and through, and his face had a light of its own and looked gaunt, like Pumpkinhead's or Skeletor's— like something you'd lock the closet on when you were young and dumb. But I told him yes because I meant it. It was a wonderful thing in its way, that scar.

He got a smoke going and stretched his legs. This was in my corner days.

Peyton used to *slang*, said Handsome.

But now I'm over that, said Peyton. Let the spooks poison themselves, I say.

But Peyton was good.

He was colonel material.

He could sell a dildo to the Virgin, someone said.

But then I got jumped and it got me to thinking, what is in this game for me? I was owning them benjamins, son, said Peyton. I was making this whole damn town my bitch. Them junkies were singing my name down on Franklin, but then another crew got keen. The way that they did me was to come up behind, just to come up behind in the dark, like this. And he mimed enfolding someone in his skinny, white arms with a phantom knife against his neck. He carved me a smile, from there to there, and I bled me a puddle about yea big. I was hooked up to tubes, on a breathing machine. Motherfucker missed the vein. Doctor said that I was lucky. One notch to the right. Peyton held up a finger. And we would be four instead of five.

And then he took his blessed time. We sat with his ass on the beep, said Handsome. We sat with him and he got well and then we got our shit together.

And we stepped up to that little bitch. We hunted him and we learned his routes. And then one night over by the abandoneds with a hooker choking on his dick, we rolled up a block or so down, in that car, and watched the glass get good and foggy. Handsome and Bo staked out, said Peyton, doing the walkie-talkie thing. And I crept round and charged my nine and peered, just so, into the window. And she is going, Guh-guh-guh. She is on his fucking stick. So I aim through the glass and pow-pow-click. The two of them get got together.

Handsome cracked up.

He killed her, too. Though I'll be fucked if I know why.

No witnesses, son. Shit was one eighty seven.

Peyton here can shoot like Pierce.

And all of a sudden I felt strange, like I'd stepped into the waters where the dragons were on maps, and the air went kind of blue and fuzzy, and I stared wide-eyed from out my skin. Peyton's was a way of being, one way among others, countless ways, and you could be like him, or you could not be, the benefit was yours to judge. But whatever his crimes, he seemed lonely to me, like the last man alive or the first one to die, and I couldn't take my eyes off him, so alien to me did he seem at that moment.

Them two deserved what they got, said Peyton.

Then he frowned and stubbed his smoke.

It was the middle of the night when we drove back through town. The only places doing business were streetlights thronged with gnats and flies. Even the stoops in our precinct were bare save a few laggard smokers too blitzed to climb stairs, and once in a while some dragon-chaser looking for a late night score, pale and unsteady and dressed for November, peering into Handsome's car. We drove through the vacated streets without braking, running our share of red lights. No one spoke. The weed and the beer had me pinned to the mat, and I struggled to keep my eyes from gluing. C.J. was looking straight ahead with considerable more than a thousand-yard stare, not too stoned to meet my eyes in the shuddering portal of the rearview, but suddenly unwilling to, like I was persona non grata, again. And then we were idling somewhere familiar, which I gradually saw was in front of my house, the boarded up windows and tumbleweed lots slow to emerge in what dimness there was, and slow to pass before the headlights, like the world was a film that had gone off its reels. The ground-floor lights of my unit were on and I winced to think upon Leander.

Thinking they meant to let me off, I took hold of the catch that would open the door, but attentions in the car contracted. I felt the torque of every stare. Handsome from driver's seat while Peyton and Bo peered in from both sides, and slowly, slowly, C.J. too, who looked at me uncertainly.

I do believe it's time, said Handsome.

But I thought that ya'll we're beyond it? I said.

None of them answered.

C.J.? I said.

Don't look at me, he said. You knew.

And the truth, I guess, was that I did.

What are you waiting for? said Peyton. This here car is going nowhere.

I'll keep her running, said Handsome. Right here.

We never leave a soldier behind, said Peyton.

A real fucking heist, shouted Bo, and slapped the ceiling. Then we divvy up the shares.

Go on, Bren. You heard, said C.J. It was me that found them anyway.

Put your hand on the door, like so, said Peyton. Give a little squeeze. Then push.

And with that the car door bounded open. The night was stale with deadened heat. Faces clustered all around me, saying things I couldn't hear.

And so I got out of the idling car, and mounted the steps of the house, and looked in, and there was Leander camped out on the couch, reading at the coffee table, mantis-like in his composure, with his head just above his impossible knees and his ankles tensed against the floor, and his finger tracing, always tracing, the words he saw before his nose, and the jerry-rigged soldier coiled there on the glass in the way that a cannibal's necklace might coil, and the four other guys waiting out in the car when I turned around to see what of them—but that was all there was, the car, hiding what was in it.

People want you to take them for granted, they do, and you do your best to give them that, but you learn over time not many deserve it, probably not even you, and the best you can do is live your life on terms you know won't disappoint you.

Without knocking once, I ran from the porch, around Handsome's car and out into the night. I guess I must've brushed his bumper, and oh, it was a souped-up piece, for both of the headlights turned on like Nightrider—like the car, tinted blind, had a life of its own. I could hear my sneakers rasping one after the next along the crud of warehouse row—low traffic tonight in that Scotch-Irish ghetto, a ghost-town of empty backyards, empty stoops. The red Toyota gunned its engine, and its wheels started up as that engine turned over, and I guess I was thinking: it's moments like these that gearheads wait for all their lives. And I thought of C.J., also, who was in the front seat, watching me grow through the hurdling glass, and I hoped for my sake he was telling them: Uncle. We only came here for them bones.

And here I was running to beat Marshall Faulk, and the neighborhood a darkened blur, and the white-hot headlights grown so big they bathed the ground five feet ahead. And I think I spread my arms, while running. And I think I thought, By God, I'm free. And I was running for a streetlight at the end of the block, the only one turned on that hour. And I was running for that streetlight, which was never getting closer, and maybe even growing dim, until the light from behind and the light up ahead merged around my running form. You see, I was trapped like a moth without wings. And that was when I turned around.

The Elder Brother
Washing His Hands

In the early hours of morning, in the State of Virginia, in the summer of 1862, a light could be seen on a dark staircase as a brother and sister ventured down. The brother's name was Grady. He was thin and wire-strung. His pale, thin face was dense with freckles. He went ahead of his sister down the stairs, bedecked in a tangle of her things: valises, petticoats, strops hung with shoes, a leatherbound brace of books. The sister, who was younger, held a candle in a dish, which lit the stairs for only her, and she picked her way down one step at a time, lifting the hem of her dress out before her, while the brother, ahead, had to toe his way down, weaving for balance between the banisters, leaning on one to shift his load and going blindly on. From a distance she appeared to descend alone, enclosed in a private haze of light, making small sounds of surprise or hesitation when her feet got ahead of her eyesight. Her brother was waiting for her at the bottom in a tight atoll of travel-things.

You walk as if you're made of glass, the brother called up through the dark to his sister.

So what if I am? she said, concentrating. Leastways I won't knock my head.

When he had her situated among her things, the brother told the sister he'd return in a minute. Going into the parlor he left her to wait beneath the grim gaze of their grandfather's portrait—he had fought in the war of 1812—a pale whiskered man decked in serge epaulets who surveyed the front hall with a tragic intensity. The girl made a game out of whipping around to catch the painting unawares or raising her candle the height of its chin and turning away in horror.

Devil take you, Grandpappy, she said, risking laughter, awaiting her brother's return.

In the parlor, the brother climbed up on the couch and parted the curtains on the drive. His father and the houseboy Aloysius were loading up the family coach, the young Negro holding a lantern hard by while the father overburdened the luggage train. The brother's older sister and mother stood near in pale but ill-considered dresses, fanning themselves against the heat like fey refugees of the season in Charleston. The Negro tracked the father at an uncertain distance and his lantern fell short of the axel-tree. The father had to feel the suitcases into place, wrenching them out when they would not fit, cursing Aloysius before plunging again beneath the raised hood of the train. When he'd found a good geometry he stood, gulping breath and let his gaze wander the house's façade, but the thick parlor curtains had since swayed to and the rest of the windows were blind with night.

Back in the foyer, the brother approached her peering up at the portrait between her raised fingers. When he touched her thin shoulder she startled around with her fingers still raised up in front of her face.

Go on outside. It's safe, he said.

You won't come, too?

I ought not, probably.

What do you mean you not ought?

I can't.

Then where are you fixing to go? she said.

Up north, I guess.

The war?

No Ma'am.

Don't call me Ma'am, she said. I'm eight.

He smiled at her pluck and smoothed her hair.

All right, Miss. Around it then. I figured I'd shimmy on by it for fun.

She stared at him intently in the dark of the hall. I do insist you write me, Grady.

I will, he said. I'll write you silly. Now get out there before you're stranded.

She took a few steps toward the door, turned around. What would the rest of them say if they knew?

Nothing pretty, he said. But you can tell them if you want to.

I won't, she said. But they might ask.

He smiled at her, weaker this time, not speaking.

What about my things? she said.

Pa'll get them, he said.

I'll ask Aloysius.

No, he said. Ask Pa.

All right.

He opened the door and stood hidden behind it, but she dawdled in the doorway with the candle in her hands.

Did the rest go to fight in the war with Cal?

Cal didn't go there to fight. He's a doctor.

Well maybe they're doctoring, too. Helping folks.

I doubt it, he said. And he hurried her forward. They've got enough trouble just helping themselves.

Can niggers be doctors like white folks can?

It's looking that way, said the brother. We'll see.

She appeared to consider this for a time. Her face was long and dull with sleep.

Go on, he said. You hear that whistle? You'll want a window seat on the way out to Auntie's.

He gently nudged her through the door and she tottered outside with the candle still lit. She looked back once, then twice, three times and turned around as if to speak, but a voice called her name and she spun and ran toward it and her candle extinguished as she ran. A thin reef of smoke hung over the drive. The brother closed the door.

He had jerried a bindle of food and loose matches to the upper brickwork of the hearth, and now he went to fetch it down and rushed through the house with it cocked on his shoulder, the rest of the rooms as dark and still as the stairs and the hallway had been. As stricken.

He slipped from the house through the kitchen's back door to a shrill explosion of cicadas, allowing its springs to bend only so far and muffling the clap of the wood with the sack. Between the kitchen door and the old slave-quarters was a stretch of twenty yards or so and the brother went half-sized through the dark, stopping sometimes on all fours in the grass to investigate the way ahead, his face now expectant, now feral by moonlight, his spine knuckled up under cloth, ankles tensed. Near the slave-quarters he crouched down again while an instance of shadow evolved on the grass. Voices came, too, growing steadily louder, voices the brother recognized, and five full-grown men sauntered out of the alley that ran between the shacks. Each of them carried an unlit torch. The brother knew this by the smell of lampoil and the sheen of the wicks in the moon. The men spoke among them in unhurried tones, though what they said he could not hear. Cyrus nudged Tom and Tom nudged back and carried the motion down to Jim and Jim, at the end, clapped Simon beside him, who muttered, Lord, Lord, and then craned to see Tom. At the back gallery of the house, they stopped. A match was struck and passed among them. One by one the torches fired and hunted along the house's trellises, showing the woodwork higher up where a Secessionist flag hung limp from the gables. But the brother did not wait to see. He had risen from his crouch and was weaving through the buildings. He turned down the alley where the men had emerged, pursued by the light of the burning porch.

Near the final outbuilding, where the property sloped and tended away into limitless trees, the brother saw a figure sitting high on a stump consumed with something in its lap. He approached with his hand fumbling at his waist for the knife he'd brought to skin his food.

I know where you going, it said.

Who's that?

Yes, sir, it said. I surely do.

The stump was chest high on the brother, and thick, with a bole at its center and squid-like roots. The legs of the figure swung down in his path, scooting the air around. They were shoeless.

Stokely? said the brother.

Yes, sir. It's me.

Then why are you crouching up there like a bobcat?

Biding my time, said the figure. Hounddogging. Hate to tell you, Marse Grady, but in case you ain't noticed your house is on fire.

I know it, he told him. I watched them set in.

Well, sir, I most sorry, but yonder she burn.

You still haven't answered my question, he said.

I ain't got a one but the one I done told.

The brother picked a match from the box in his bindle and dragged it to life down the side of the tree. Within its flare, the Negro sat, wood-shavings piled in his lap. He'd been whittling.

We a sorrowful whip scared lot, said Stokely. Can't blame us much for the houses we burn.

I don't, said the brother. I believe it's your time.

Stokely laughed softly. Yes, sir. It seem so.

The match had burned down to the brother's finger-pads. He shook it dead and let it drop.

So where is it you think I'm headed?

Darksome path, Lord bless you, sir.

And you're on the path to that freedom, I reckon?

The Negro whistled, kicked his legs. Close as I can get, he said.

Aren't they alike, just dressed up different?

Young Marse got powerful notions, he do.

I go where I'm needed, he said. And you?

You go where you think you is needed, said Stokely.

And who's to say I'm not? he said.

I know for sure you ain't, said Stokely.

They were silent a moment. They heard the house raging. The flickering stain of the firelight crept towards them like something intent on their blood through the woods.

Reckon you'll move on tomorrow? he said.

Move on something fierce, said Stokely.

Best loot the house ere it goes, said the brother.

He could feel Stokely searching his eyes in the dark.

Yes, sir, he said. I'll pass the word.

Good luck to you, Stokely, he said and reached out.

But the Negro had moved down off the stump and stood out of range of the brother, staring at him. He stared at him a moment more and then he walked away.

The brother walked to Maryland because he knew that the war would be there to greet him. He forsook the state road where his family had gone and where his eldest brother had gone before them, a road that ran north and then forked east up the kindly plateaus at the hem of the mountains, and one that would have brought him across the state line with a minimum of danger. He was for the mountains that would cradle him up to the top of the state as far as Leesburg, and there, at the mouth of the Potomac River, he could follow the fighting north. They were thin and ragged mountains, like the spine of a lizard, and riddled with spruces peak to base. The brother gained a ridge where he crouched, chewing bread, and watched his birthright smolder in the valley below, the wind drawing huge bloats of smoke up the cut that broke on the base of the mountains. In the blueness of dawn, the fire burned brighter; an island of flame, impossibly orange. He could see figures milling in the field, among the shacks, and within sparking distance of the fire, in three groups. No one there came on with water. Pity the man who would have tried. The last potential water-bearers had quit that place the night before.

Then the brother noticed a trio of figures who were walking away from the fire, right toward him. They were dark and anonymous as the shrubs that grew downgrade of the ridge where he crouched, and they moved in a processional, one by one, in a manner ceremonial and militant both. He watched them make across the fields and across the plateaus to the mouth of trail, but did not wait to watch them climb for fear of being spotted. He shouldered his bindle, stretched, and went on, up the rock-studded spine of the mountains.

Night of her birth, a violent storm. Rain sluicing off the eaves, down the gutters. Full-throated wind in the crowns of the oaks. The moon behind the driving rain like an oracle's face behind bead curtains, hanging. Prayer songs ascending to queer his young ears from out the doorways of the shacks, soothing the blood-wails of difficult labor, the drumline of the falling rain. Then sudden silence. Hallelujah's and Hosannah's. Clamor in a distant room. The stooped Negro doctor emerged in his shirtsleeves, treasured the newborn aloft to the storm.

Near to dawn he stopped to rest in a scarce plot of grass by the side of the trail. He had not been eating nor had he been drinking in accord with the strain that his travels took on him, and his decision to rest, just one day out, was one that his flesh had made out of necessity. He fell into slumber so intense it seemed refined of even dreams, and when he awoke in the bright afternoon it was only with considerable effort. But scarcely had he forced his eyes than roiling dust convulsed them shut. A confusion of horses' hooves stormed past; he rolled over sneezing to cover his face. When at last he was able to see shapes again: a horseman above him, tin-stamped on the light.

He was one of a company of six, the other five waiting ahead in the trail. He was grizzled, red-eyed, unwashed to negritude. His hat looked like something long dead in the road.

What's your company? he said.

The brother coughed. I'm not enlisted.

Want to be?

No, but I thank you.

All right.

The horseman spit, removed his hat and clawed his fingers through his hair.

We're going to rendezvous with Lee. Most of us joined up this morning. Say, what's your business round this way if it ain't with them blue-suited mott-lickers North?

I'm hunting somebody.

Blue feller or grey?

Neither, really, said the brother.

No such thing as that these days. All us got to take a side.

Then, technically he's blue, he said. He's doctoring under McClellan.

How's that different, to your thinking?

Not a lot different, I guess. It's complex.

Sounds pretty simple. Your man's a backslider.

It's personal business between him and me.

Well, said the horseman. My offer's still good. If you've a mind to, you can ride on with us.

The brother nodded sharply. I thank you, but no.

The horseman watched him for a moment. How are you for food and drink?

I've still got a couple of mile's worth yet.

The horseman grinned and shook his head in a sort of wondrous disbelief. He took out his canteen and dislodged the stopper and passed to the brother, who nodded his thanks.

Good luck to you, then, said the man, while he drank. I'll commend your stupidity on to the General.

The brother stopped the canteen and handed it up. I'll commend it to him on my own, if I see him.

Long live the south, said the horseman.

All right.

And long live brothers of the cause. The horseman gave pause. Are you at least one of those?

Hard put to decide just yet.

Well come on to Maryland when you do. We'll skewer some Yankee dogs together.

He tipped his hat and toed his mount and rode in haste to gain his fellows who were all five advancing in close single-file along the high bluffs to the east.

The brother surveyed the country round. His legs had done well for him thus far. The staggered rock-faces, the spruce-choked gulleys, and the narrow mountain passes of the land he had crossed looked ugly and fierce, inconceivably treacherous. Yet there were the figures, ranked and solemn, sure-footed as goats on the lower escarpment, making across the ground he'd covered with a grace that suggested their feet never touched. A family of Negroes who had not stayed to watch their prison fall to ashes, or perhaps refugees from the languishing guard, old knights of the South who had traded their linen for a penitent's cloth befitting the hour. And the brother could see now it was day that they were cowled from head to toe, and that the one in the middle was shorter than the others, its vestments dragging on the ground. They seemed to be walking in remembrance of something, though what this was he could not say.

I see you, the brother said. Can whoever it is you are see me?

Congruent upbringings, his and hers. He in the house and her house in the thickets. Butterfly chases and firefly hunts throughout the milder of the seasons, he among the trellised bougainvillia and wisteria, she among the kudzu and the weeds between the shacks. Mason jars and corkboard squares, perched in like arrangements on their windowsills and bedsteads. She of the explosive hair, skin cooked smooth like exposed saddle-leather. He of the cowlick, unaccustomed white hands, well-fed rolls above the belt. Aunt Berenice, his soft Negro Mammy, making out the limits of his play on the lawn. Sometimes Margaret with him too, driving her shadow abreast of his own, while Cal sat collected and strange on the porch, learning his anatomy. She with her mother Antoinette in whatever hours the woman was afforded for this office, her little brother Stokely capering through the tall grass, clapping his small cushioned hands. One light and one dark, each observing the other, across a field of nascent cotton.

That night he came into a dry, wooded valley that lay in the void between two mountains. A place where moonlight could not reach, and by that logic sunlight neither, for the trees were arthritic, the shrubs desiccated, the ground as barren as a pan. Mindful of the local character, he found himself drawing in shallower breaths. The trees were more tangled the further he went, growing all which ways but up—and in the absence of moonlight, a soft phosphorescence seemed to rise up from the ground. Up ahead, a sort of throne made by two embroidered oaks, from the low boughs of which hung a cast-off robe that the brother only noticed when it brushed along his forearm. He stopped in the darkness and fingered the robe and made to pass between the trees, but the voice of a woman spoke his name from the black recesses of the throne. He froze.

Grady Earl Coontz, the strange voice said. Rest your bones a while with me.

I'll rest your bones, he said. Who's there?

Now the voice did not respond. He approached the wooden throne with his knife at the ready. An ancient woman sat cross-legged, faintly luminous, like an idol in a niche. She was totally nude, very pale in the ground-light. Withered paps and ropy arms. White hair parted either side of her face like a thicket she'd emerged from. Behind her long and knotty head, a hulking armature of spine, as if she harbored in her frame a pair of mighty blackened wings. A foul archangel cursed to walk. Or was he cursed to walk with her?

The brother asked the canopy, Am I asleep by any chance?

But the woman was real, for the woman was speaking.

The Vengeful are ugly, in thought and in deed. Share we this, in spite of age, in spite of origin and sex, in spite of sundry opposites that present circumstances vex, and thus am I disposed this night to speak to you of what may come that you might come yourself, and soon, to curse the day or see it won. For Vengefulness will take you far, from mountains high to valleys low, through heat unholier than Hell's and darkness darker yet than death, across doldrums where no winds blow, and through limbos of life bereft. Despite dead men laid in your path, and war-scarred regions in your wake, where fires burn and structures lean such as the fire could not break. Against the omens of we three, your vengefulness will drive its prow, and trammel too your soul's unease, or such of it you will allow. But be you vehicle of hate, or architect of just design, I cannot say, for know I not. This shall you yourself define.

You could just as well save me the trouble, he said. Or the headache of listening to you, at that. He scrubbed at his face with his palms and stepped back. Now I'm going to blink my eyes.

When he opened his eyes, the hag was gone. So too the tree-branch of her robe. He was crouched absurdly in the alcove, scarring the wood of the tree, like a lover, when suddenly the moon appeared to show him where he was.

He walked through the night and through the coolness of the morning until the land greened before leveling out, and he dozed the hottest of the day in a sheltering thicket of spruce, un-dreaming. He woke as the last of the afternoon sun was threading itself between the trees and he rose with the sweat still drying on his face. Leaves and dirt clung to his cheeks. Sore feet. He ate a bleak sandwich of white bread and chocolate, rationing sips from his canteen to chase it.

On a ledge of limestone by the side of the trail he stood to watch the sun's decline, and the valley below seemed a volcanic waste in the brilliance of the moment when it dropped behind the hills. Going across the lower climes was the band of pursuers diminished by one; a twosome now, one tall, one short, their shadows gliding on the rocks and extending before them like tattered familiars. The hag was no longer among them, it seemed, if she had ever been at all, for when he reflected on last night's events they seemed to him likelier ones he had dreamed. And indeed, sometimes, the figures wavered, grew closer to him and then more distant, seemed solid enough to block the light that wrought their shadows on the ground and yet other times seemed shadows themselves, projected up slant from the earth of their making. He wondered again if they were real and then he wondered did it matter.

I'll be waiting for you, the brother said. Pebbles skipped off the trail's edge—he had kicked them. I'll be waiting for you. He was shouting it now. The cliffs either side pitched his voice back.

Tragedy in his fourteenth year when his Bay, Thurgood, tore a hole in the fence, half-disembowling itself in the process. The ragged edges of its belly where it had failed to clear the jump. Eyes rolling white and muzzle frothing for him to deliver it peace. But he could not. Him sitting down among the leakage, smoothing its fearful ears flush, crooning to it. She emerging from the shacks, not thirteen years old, but attuned to his misery. A harrow cradled in her arms, sharp edge shining down the furrows.

Are you all right?

My horse is done for.

I see that. Are you all right?

Now that she was here with him. But he did not say so, just stared. Inordinate beauty for only one soul. Hair a mist above her head, copper in the afternoon. A larking sad wisdom at large in her eyes, confusing the feeling they rendered in him.

I brought this here for you. He's hurt.

I don't think I can do what you're saying I've got to.

But you've got to, she said. It's the right thing to do.

I know, he said, but I just can't.

Then I'll help you, she told him and offered the harrow.

On three, she said.

Say, ten.

No, three.

How old are you?

I'm twelve, she said.

You're keen for twelve.

So I've been told.

Eyes meeting briefly, then shying away.

Where do I? he said.

Right here.

You're sure?

I think.

You *think?* he said.

She smiled and touched the horses' temple. In the small beating heart of the fur there, all life.

What's your name? he said.

It's June.

I'm Grady, he said.

I know your name.

In the higher altitudes, things greened. Creepers, kudzu, weeping willows, Japanese wisteria. It was the middle of the night but it might have been noon for all the unique smells and birdcall. Lilies-of-the-valley by the side of the trail like diminutive ghosts in the haze of the moon as it washed about the brother's ankles, and though he'd passed through worse ground-fog amidst the valley of the hag, this kind was milky, sweet-smelling, unnatural. It made the brother plug his nose. But the fauna did not seem to mind. Hare and foxes streaked the trail. And owls made mastery of the heights. And rodents tunneled through the bramble, fleeing from death on the wing. And then he saw a pile of them who were swarming and feeding on something enormous, a creature at least ten times their size that was made indistinct by the bevvy of plant-life, but one that the brother could only assume would've hunted them down in a right-side-up world. The rodents moved over the hump of dead meat like automata on a shuttle, pausing to chisel and thrash with their faces between the fastness of its bones.

After a while he came into a clearing which was just a slim crescent among the trees. At the opposite end, its back to him, a figure rooted in the dirt. About the size of a child were it not for its head, which he gauged, at a glance, twice the size of his own. It appeared to be digging something up, digging something under, or maybe just digging. The muscles of its naked back were dense and electric with strain.

The child-sized figure noticed him. A queer feral jerk of the head, waist twisting, hands curling up at its chest, like a lizard's. He thought that it would spit at him, but then it drew upright.

The child stared at him for a time. The brother stared back, a bit sick in his stomach. Its head was so huge that it might have belonged to a heftier child who now went around headless. Below the neck it was hairless, and below the waist sexless, with thin, double-jointed-looking legs, like a foal's. Its eyes were coin-sized pools of black without any iris to speak of.

The thing made a dash for a nearby tree and scurried up among the boughs. It took up a crouch, staring down the brother, with its long toes twisted around the branch. The mouth in its face, when it opened to speak, was a perfectly black and toothless hole.

I was never born, but am. And I follow on the heels of the Vengeful, for she made me.

It had a high and burbling voice, like a deaf and dumb child crying out underwater.

I'm sorry to hear that, said the brother, and started to approach the tree, but the child disappeared in a chaos of leaves and emerged through a parting five feet higher up.

Vengefulness will take you far and long sustain you with its heat. So far have you come, Young Coontz, and two of us yet chanced to meet. But Vengeance is a second savored, perpetrated in half that, so weigh you carefully its merits before you serve it, tit for tat. But alas where Vengefulness propels, Vengeance must needs issue forth, so who are we, mere agents three, to reroute you upon your course? Which brings us to the hour of Vengeance, verily, an hour of death, though in your case, midst war and waste, death, like blood, will call to death. Indeed, Vengeance may warp and pale, as I have warped and paled myself, though hasten judgment must we not, humble agents three, one less. And yet less two, now I have spoke; our last remaining minion comes. Recognize his face will you by the fact that he has none.

Slowly, the brother shook his head. His palms, outstretched, began to tremble. And then with a howl of disbelief that had the while been boiling in him, he ran to the base of the tree, where he stopped. The child's face was gone and the canopy dark. There was only a tossing of shadowy boughs to suggest it had been there at all.

Through the following day, a poisonous heat. Mirages of water and shade on the trail. Gnats and mosquitoes, in the nighttime voracious, wallowing by in disinterested arcs. Every half-mile the brother stopped to wipe off the sweat from his brow with his shirtfront. He had taken to turning around when he did this to count the miles that he had come, although he had promised himself before leaving that this was what he would not do. But he stopped to count the miles regardless, subtracting them from the miles ahead, and found he was either too close to the war or too far from home to turn back.

He went along a mountain pass where there was barely room to walk. The trail spiraled upwards, and then funneled down, as if undecided which way it should tend. Going around another bend, a pair of feet amidst the trail. On closer inspection it was one of the company that the brother had met on his second day out, this ragged stranger dead for days, with none but the flies grouped there in remembrance. The man's leg was swollen to outlandish dimensions; suggestive, he thought, of an untended wound, or a run-in with a deadly snake. There were coins upon his sightless eyes, though one of them slightly less in value, as if those who he rode with had emptied their pockets, unable to find two coins the same. The brother read the man's name tag. Ennis McHolister Sage, it said.

The corkscrew passage channeled straight at what the brother judged to be the summit of the ranges, and now the sun was cooking into twilight below, he stopped for a while to feel breeze on his face. The last and tallest of the figures was making up the grade behind him with a slow and effortless locomotion, with nothing whatsoever of the clumsiness of man. Its black robe fluttered out behind it with such voluminosity it might have been wings, or a dark ectoplasm that it labored at the center of, bearing it up against gravity's custom.

The brother hailed the figure. Ho, there. It did not waver. Ho, there, he repeated, you laggard spook. But then it was lost to the hills.

He went on.

From Thurgood's death onward, contrary polarities. He fascinated, then enraptured by her, this siren of the garden hanging laundry out to dry, or by the river of an evening with the other washerwomen as they slapped out the bedding from soaking to damp. No rest for these laundresses, these shiners of brass, these fillers of decanters and platers of meals. No more than there was for the lovesick, this boy, crouched among trees for a fleetness of thigh, or for the quiver of a backside through the cloth of a dress.

Hello June, he would say.

Marse Grady, she'd answer.

Your hair looks plenty fine in braids.

I thank you, Marse.

No need. And it's Grady.

Well, I thank you Marse. Most girls got braids.

Days of her kneeling in the garden, skirts hitched up past her knees while she weeded. Nights of her passing through the rooms, on this or that errand in the hours before sleep, when the fires stretched their spines on the manicured hearths and the kerosene lamps burned low in their niches. Cal taking notice along with him much to the detriment of his studies, and the two brothers rising from their chairs, or craning around where they stood to observe her, or shadowing her, even, at the minutest distance, as if they themselves were unaware of desiring her, for they often found themselves within an inch of her person, mutually blind as to how they had got there, or wherefore they had been propelled, knowing only that here was a creature to contemplate, and with her, a whole way of life. Cal putting down his anatomy book and sliding his pince-nez down his nose, the same two motions every evening—and to think the brother noticed neither.

June pretending not to see, but not unwelcome to it, either, this awkward foolish, forthright passion that Cal had conceived for the house nigger's daughter, and one that he planned to see out to its end, little had the brother known. And then when Chestnut hit Fort Sumter and Cal suited blue as he'd promised he would, the younger brother ran to find him, wanting to ask him was he scared, wanting, again, to hear the why of why he would not fight for Dixie. Not just Cal he found, however, bursting unannounced into the parlor off the kitchen, having searched every inch of the house and the grounds and this, the one place he'd not looked. Hair, her hair, pressing under the shelf where the sacks of biscuit flour were lined, and Cal was driving up inside her, using the backs of her shoulders for leverage. Even worse, the brother felt, was that he could not see her face. In the moment their crisis came upon them Cal clapped his hand over her mouth, and then with the other one clutching her stomach he guided her through their cycling down. The brother watching them with such immense force of feeling that gradually they turned around. But the brother had gone—was out walking the fields and walking through the bloody cotton, with the image of their violent coupling returning to gall him again and again. There in the drive when he got back, his brother's midnight coach departing, and nothing from Cal in the way of farewell but what he had seen in the parlor that night. Forms at the edge of the slave barracks, watching, murmuring among themselves.

Along northern ridges, long views of the country. Forsaken tracts of farmland, grotesquely overgrown. Wooden plows appointed to stand in the corn like pointless contraptions of torture. Along a spine of shale he crept. Pebbles trickling down the grade, the rough, rusty sound of his breath in his throat and now a dry wind in among the birch-boughs the only natural sounds in hearing. Soon the air went dim with smoke that densened and darkened down the valley and suggested low fires that could never be glimpsed for the sheer amount of smoke they spewed, and lo it appeared from where he stood that smoke was arising right out of the earth, as though the Yanks had gone so far as to set their blazes at its core. What land he could see through the rifts in the smoke was vaingloriously ravaged after Carthage or Cannae, with the furrows tossed and leveled, and in places scorched fallow, and with the galleried houses and outbuildings chewed and ransacked to their girders. Even the gaunt, sporadic slums that leaned from the hills surrounding the houses had been met with the same itinerant violence. And not a soul in sight.

A night to redefine the word. Black and still beyond all reckoning. So dark, in fact, that he began to disbelieve in the world he had witnessed by daylight. Branches, shrubs, and hanging moss made a gauntlet of the trail, but the brother tore free of their claws and loped on without nothing but his fear to guide him.

Then he passed a curious shape. At first he took it for a birch with uncommonly white, reflective skin, but then he saw there was no moon, so how could it be shining? On closer inspection, it was a man, standing idly in his path. Or maybe not idly, the brother considered, for the man was too rigid to be without purpose, and seemed to be keen to the coming of something, there in the limitless dark. To make matters stranger, he appeared to be blind, for he did not mark the brother coming, and he stood with an aspect of blindness about him, listing slightly to one side.

The man addressed him: Grady Coontz. Come and stand a while with me.

So you're number three, I expect? said the brother.

Indeed, said the man, with a nod. I am he.

He was in a sorry state of nature. Piebald chest and withered shanks. And when the brother came in close he discovered the face was entirely featureless. While the body was that of a very old man, the struts of him collapsed and slack, the face was like a wall of gauze; he could scarcely imagine the source of the voice. The horrid figure's cast-off robe had been spread on the ground beneath its feet, and here he stood, as on a dais, suspended in the element around him.

Where Vengefulness will drive you long, and Vengeance satiate your gall, it is I, the Avenged, at cycle's end, who shows withal an inkless page, upon whose regions yet are writ the dicta of one damned or saved. For the Avenged, his hatred slaked, or thirsting still within his breast, may live to see his enemy against all odds become a friend. But lo for pride he will see lost a part of him to which blood beats, and taste of his hypocrisy with all nature imparts, one less. The path remaining wants your toe. Or else the path behind your heel. Give it fore or aft, young Coontz. Smear the wax or the plant the seal.

It passed a hand over its face to illustrate the blankness there, and shadow fingers dribbled down a beat behind the hand that made them.

At once the forest bloomed with moonlight. Footlamps reigniting on a vaudeville stage. The trees revealed themselves as such, then the shrubs and hanging moss. The man without a face was gone, though where the brother could not guess, for certainly one so strange as he had no way to live among men unmolested; materializing, prophesying, standing naked in the dark, preceded always by the hag and the malformed child—for him the brother felt, at once, a sort of misdirected pity, but not a smidgeon for himself, because what was he doing standing there with such a distance left to cover? But he stood there for a good while longer, pivoting dreamily in the glade, wondering not what he should do, but how he should go about doing it.

First weeks of Cal's absence, the summer in earnest. The bushes releasing their berries, all skin. Lovesickness, boredom and bitter frustration became for him states cooked down by heat into one paranoid master-state, and caused him to appear to lurk even in places natural for him to be in. She, hurrying through the fog of his stare, sometimes with a frank disgust, so that occasionally he'd order her to clean or to mend things just to hear her acquiesce. In the meanwhile came letters she could not read but that she got the old doctor to read aloud to her, and then in the halting, emotionless tone of one accustomed only to reading prescriptions and procedurals from outdated medical books so the elder's account of doctoring for McClellan had all the impact of a Sunday school pamphlet. The younger intercepting now, at first experimentally, and then as a rule. As glad of the elder's pronouncements of love as he was of the hardship and trauma of war, because he could not decide which brought him more pleasure, to feel his hatred justified or to know his older brother suffered, and since the letters dealt in both, he read and reread them again and again. And abusing those letters more practically now, not for their content, but places of origin, plotting the postmaster's seal from each city in between predictions from the Herald in town, and when he could get it, The Richmond Dispatch, as to which way the tide of war would presently pitch its bulk and when. These latter marks with headless pins, the former with ones studded black to mean certainty. Courses emerging like spirit-trails across the map's contested regions. To cross the hills to meet with Lee, or around the base of them to melt in with Hood? Then, on a day when she stood cleaning plates at the big metal sink that abutted the scullery, he came up behind her, encircled her waist and buried his nose in her hair.

No, Marse Grady. Ain't what you think. Ease off now, she said. Ease back.

But him clinging to her, absorbing her smell, such a rare, garden smell, but also mammalian. He could not remove his poor, drunk nose from the hair at the base of her skull. So she levered herself around to face him and launched from the sink to drive him back. Telling him: Off. Get off, I said. Which was left reverberating in the kitchen. Releasing her startled, ashamed, enraged. Abandoned the kitchen for some place she wasn't but no place existed, he found soon enough. Stumbling around for the rest of the day, he forgot to intercept the mail and with it a letter from his brother, the fifth unanswered of its kind, calling for her to quit the house and join him in Kentucky.

The brother reached Sharpsburg just after dawn, on the fourteenth day of his journey. The woods outside the town had smoke, and the bloody percussion of cannons and muskets could be heard in the cornfield beyond. Only where the woods thinned out did the brother encounter the first of the fallen. They lay in the dirt in a grim disarray, blue coats and grey coats alike and unbreathing— some of them prone, and some face-up, and some who slumped, their backs to trees, in parliaments of wordless sorrow. He found no living soul among them. Muskets and cavalry swords lay strewn. He fetched himself a stray Enfield, began to creep around the corn. Then, ahead of him, small drama. Two boys tussling in the leaves. One of them blue, brass-buttoned, bugle-hatted, with a rusty blue sash around his waist, and the other one not grey, per se, but clearly allied with the stripe of that army, for the rags that he wore had been leached of their color like the grave cerements of a beggar. They were strangely isolated from the battle at large, in a glade where the sun filtered down among the trees, and the brother crouched down to watch their struggle with a look of scientific curiosity. Too close to charge muskets and fire with any accuracy, they had opted for their bayonets, and were currently locked in an awkward seesaw with the bores of the muskets pitted tensely together, their boyish arms shaking with the strain of the impasse and their dirty faces twisted up. Trading curses back and forth as to which would be off to the Summerland first. But if either of them knew what the other one threatened, the brother would be damned—they were children. The Yankee boy slipped in a silk of pine needles and the Reb, caught off balance, slipped forward in turn, whereon the blade of the latter sank into the former, and he fell with the gun sticking out of his gut. But because of the suddenness of his kill the Reb fell, contagiously, right along with him and after a moment of dangling high in a pantomime of schoolboy antics, the Reb took his hands from the butt of his gun and pitched over south with a startled expression. In the following silence, while the Union boy died, both of them sat in the dirt.

By the time he reached the Union line, his ears were wretched with the noise. No one paid him any mind, Confederate though he might have been, as if any man mad enough to reconnoiter with such a traffic of lead in the air as there was would have the wits nor wherewithal to sabotage their camp. He watched a Union volley and a Rebel response, hasty and smoke-blinded shots to the man. Gaps appeared across both lines as men knelt silent in the dirt while the cavalry horses reared and plunged, trying to buck their cursing riders. Cannons also broke the lines, dispersing men's heads, raining dirt upon others, while the officers aft of these unlucky few spurred themselves around the flank and glassed the field to count the fallen. The center of the field was a smoky limbo where only the stubble of cornstalks remained.

He passed along the rampart with his commandeered gun like a child in a spirit photograph and as silent, while all around him muskets flashed and men fell down the whole field over. Since there was little correspondence between shots fired and men who fell before the shots, death was occurring in no right pattern and the skirmish seemed to happen much slower than it did. A smoothbore bucked from Rebel climes, furrowing the Union flank, and a dirty red fog of what once had been men hung thick for a time over those there remaining—and these, the favored, in their turn, wiped smears of their brethren away and marched on. And a corpsman broke formation running forward with his musket in a fog of violence so intense that he scarcely resembled a man any longer with his mouth twisted wide, and his dark eyes agog, and his limbs swinging crazily all which ways yet stopped in his charge when he saw, looking down, that one of his legs had deserted him. And there was a Reb on the opposite side who careened like a drunk amidst the smoke while his fellows tried to pass him to the margins of the battle for the shrapnel-wedge lodged in his neck but they couldn't—like the Yank without a leg, he was cordially trampled, and the brother could not see what happened to him after that. But mostly Rebs and Yanks alike were picked apart by minié balls until they were but racks of bone to which sinew and vitals clung, left there to teeter among the scorched corn like mutilated scarecrows.

It was only when a carbine chewed into an oak after shaving along his hairless check that the brother came back to himself and remembered the bedlam in which he'd fetched up.

For then, behind breastworks and off among trees, the brother saw a medic's tent. There were men queued up for fifteen yards to gain admittance at the flap. They were short legs or arms, had been gored in the ears; they were terribly burned or disfigured by shrapnel. For every man who went inside there were three carried out by the feet or on stretchers, most of them dead and others close to it who gibbered old names that no one knew, or tried to make their peace with God. The brother sat against a spruce with the musket bridged over his knees and waited. After a while he took up the gun and started to load it as best as he recalled. He cloth-wrapped the cartridge and jimmied it down, once and then two times, with the ramrod; he pressed the primer into place, then dusted the barrel and breach with gunpowder. He hefted the gun and drew a bead on an adolescent bugler to the left of the tent, but when the boy walked out of range he propped it stock-first in the ground at his feet.

A man in a bloody surgeon's apron parted the flap of the tent and stepped out to direct the flow of traffic inward. The brother stared intently at this man, who was distant. He reassessed his weapon's readiness. The man had the same thinnish face as the brother but increased by a long and imperious chin; and the same long muscles as him, too, but slightly less slapdash and twisted together. He made more sense in his skin overall. His apron was dyed to the hem with blood and he held in his right hand a bright bonesaw that he absently started to gesture with, indicating to a corporal where the dead men should go, where the fatally wounded, where the barely intact, three different camps up ahead in the trees that were staffed, the brother saw, by yet other surgeons. The corporal nodded at him and the man spoke onward. The corporal seemed to hang on his every word. When the man was done speaking they just stood there and regarded one another through the thick drifts of smoke, their worn, dirty figures hunched in on themselves, and their faces very pale.

The brother drew a bead on the man in the apron. He cocked the hammer into readiness. His hands began to shake the muzzle. So he stood it in dirt and he raised it again.

Goddamn you, you meddling spooks. He canted his aim to the left and fired.

The shot carried wide of the man with the chin. A puncture marred the canvas tent. The man looked around at the sound of the rip but the one who had fired was concealed by the trees, and the corporal, who was halfway in front of the man as if to take the bullet for him, had instinctively drawn his long carbine and described the clearing with it. The brother reloaded without meaning to. It was all he could think to do at the moment. The corporal advanced across the grass to see about this hidden scout.

A pretty Negro woman came out of the tent and reached awkwardly for the man in the apron. She was wearing an apron herself, just as bloody; her hair was tied up in an old ragged scarf. The woman reached and reached again, a frail, stunted motion, like the gathering of air—but devil how close in she got, and devil how she spread her arms, it was never close or wide enough, as if she were poised on a spindle. The brother saw she could not stand, was staggering with the effort to, her arms not level at her sides but clutched around her aproned ribs. She started to fall, past the man with the chin, who turned around and caught her up. He tried to make her stand but she would not. So he laid her to grass and he knelt down above her.

When he saw her, the brother abandoned his musket and walked automatically out from the trees. He walked despite the snooping corporal, who had judged his position from the shot. The man had a Spencer repeating rifle. He riddled the brother's whole left side. The brother veered crazily on his path and fell into the thin, scorched grass. He stared across the clearing with a long, titled view of the girl where she lay near the mouth of the tent, but the boots of the corporal stomped into view. The man's dirty face, with its trailing mustaches, leaned over close into his.

Hand of war stings a good bit, don't it, son? Sure can deal you backhand, he said.

When the brother lost consciousness his left side was numb, but a numbness that promised great pain, given time. The last thing he saw were the corporal's hands lowering onto his collar.

He woke in the murk of the medical tent with the man in the apron positioned above him. The man was looking at him with profound concentration, as if he could not make him out. The brother's dim surroundings swam in a viscous and yellow preservative agent—an infant with a freak of spine marooned inside a bulbous jar. The hot metallic scent of blood was the first thing he smelled when the murk finally cleared. Next came the gunfire and wails and horse-screams of the battle still happening somewhere close by him. And finally the pain itself in searing runs along his arm and in among his battered ribs, as if a starved creature were eating its way from the top of his shoulder down into his guts.

The brother lurched up on his palette. He gripped—had been gripping—the aproned man's wrist.

I was aiming for you. I missed, he said.

You never were much of a shot, said the man.

Where is she laid up? he said. She's got to be all right. She's got.

When the aproned man said nothing and continued to stare, the brother did a shallow laugh.

You're sparing me—well, don't, he said. I don't need to be protected.

First things first, he said. That arm. It's got to go soon if you want to keep breathing.

The brother let his eyes drift down to where his arm, a cob, was lying. Portions of bone were showing through, glaringly white, with a finely wrought grain. There was a big swath of cotton soaking blood on his ribs and bandages layered around and around him to keep the pressure constant.

When this arm is gone, I will still have the other. And men have done worse, with just one arm. Besides, said the brother, eyes softening some. To let me off easy's the worst you can do.

If it gladdens your twisted sense of right, I reckon I'll go it without anesthetic.

You do that, the brother said. And wake me up if I pass out.

Though he seemed on the verge of responding to this, the man in the apron shook his head. He set the freezing saw-teeth in a deep groove of muscle just below the brother's shoulder. When the brother looked up he was gritting his teeth and tearing up a little in the corners of his eyes. But the man regained composure with a powerful stroke that freckled his face and smock with blood.

He woke to a blackness that hemorrhaged faint light, and then before him rose the world. He was inside some sort of room, perhaps the same one as before, and lay on what he now discerned was some manner of medic's cot; he scanned the dim, astringent room for something else to take his bearings, but all he saw were supine figures half-submerged in pale blue light. His posture felt off and he looked himself over. A mummified stump where his left arm had been. He willed the stump twitch, and it did. He lay back. Then sat up again. He was sweating profusely. A dull, diffuse pain, or the specter of pain, was running up and down his side. He lowered his feet to the floor with a grimace, settled himself against a stake and strategically leaned left-right, right-left, to get a sense for his new equilibrium. He emerged from the tent on a crutch at his right, a Union issue blanket cowled about him in the heat. Woodsmoke and gunsmoke and spirits and blood encumbered the air now the battle was through. The field was hot, festooned with bugs and windless as a bayou.

Medics of both allegiances trolled through the slaughter on foot or by deadcart, scaring up weapons for redistribution. They collected stray rations, compasses, telescopes, spurs, saddle-winches, shot-pouches, horseshoes, odds and ends of uniforms as small as gold braids, brass buttons and tassel, or as integral as riding boots, cavalry jackets and three-cornered hats. The soldier's kit they tossed en mass into huge sacks hanging over their shoulders and with uneaten rations, too, and with the talismans men clutched they let their consciences contend, for there was many a man among their party who knelt to bite an unclaimed ring or to slip a fob-watch from a cavalry jacket and twine it around his wrist, with four others. Weaving among their legs went hogs and scurvied dogs and plume-tailed foxes, flirting with the meals that they would make of the unburied before the day was out.

The brother watched these scavengers, cold despite the heat. One-armed and lucky to be, all considered. And expected to see among these men, resplendent in their robes of doom, the hag and the child and the faceless man come to claim his soul. But they were nowhere. He looked for them and looked for them, scanning the field twice over, then thrice. He scanned the medics, then the dead, then the field officers smoking their pipes beneath canvas tents pitched along the perimeter, then the haggard infantry fanning themselves, crouched in their blood-stiffened clothes, drinking coffee, while a chaplain in his wide blue sash gathered some men around for prayer. And here was his brother, crouched over a bucket, washing the blood from his hands in the dawn. They were the hands of a surgeon, strong and dexterous, twice the size of Grady's own. He was watching the battlefield in profile, not aware of Grady yet and he seemed to see nothing but what was in front of him: the humdrum blasphemy of war. But what else did he see in that broad killing field? What manner of angel? What manner of man? What did he see that his brother could not, who now crutched back inside the tent? His brother, who lay on his cot in the heat and tried to fathom what he'd done.

Albino Deer

He was nineteen years old and 6'3". His skin was the bronze shade of watercourse piping. He wore a black leather vest-piece with fringe on the bottom after the fashion of hair-metal frontmen and his waist-length black hair he tied up in a ponytail, or on dressier days in two thick braids. His Grandmother was full Cherokee, a fact that he flaunted to girls and older men, and to heighten the fact liked to carry himself with an air of aggrieved nobility. He'd successfully avoided all his life a comprehensive study of the ways of his ancestors, and had cobbled up a notion of who he should be from the hearsay of ignorant whites. For him it was a point of pride that Cherokee men withstood their whiskey, laid their lives' plans by the span of the moon, tracked every meal they hoped to eat in a hand-me-down pair of rawhide chaps, the shards of obsidian in their boots the only acceptable means of bloodletting. If corrected, he would say he'd co-opted these notions to give his enemies a taste, as if feeding a man with his own fool misconceptions were a surefire way to make him learn. His name was William Henry Shaw, a curious one for a half-breed, he thought, though in truth he was only a quarter. He had graduated high school with very few prospects and at his father's urging had taken a job at the General Store in town.

The store was open twenty-three hours a day. William came on at eight in the morning to help his boss Singleton scrub down the grill that they used to fry up eggs and meat. The store would reopen for business at nine. William sat there on an old wooden stool whose seat, all these years beneath Singleton's ass, had molded to the shape of it. He greeted the daily ebb and flow. He counted out the register.

He sectioned invoices by date and delivery and attacked, like a maniac wielding a nail-gun, whole shipments of freezer-stiff goods with his labeler. He serviced the antique popcorn machine that Singleton warned him would jam and catch fire the moment William had his back turned. It had once, he said, in a vicious blaze, and the store had shut down for a week. He'd suffered losses. If William was going to lift a finger then it might as well be to protect his own skin, for not only would he be sacked if the store went up on William's watch but William might well lose his life so the better to suffer some burns on his knuckles than be both dead and jobless.

Walking home after work to the one-story house that he shared with his father, a winey old roofer, William watched the traffic pass. Greyhound buses moaning through, muscle cars with drunken captains, the tragic hatchbacks of the other night people: waitresses, watchmen, janitors, William. Sometimes pickups, jeeps and vans with figureheads of bloody meat, deer and moose and even foxes lashed to the trunk or the roof. He envisioned confrontations with the passengers, all. There would be an event that would draw them together. And William, throughout the course of this, would be in the right, no matter his role. Home at night he beat his pillow in sweaty pantomimes of vengeance, more gratified than he knew he should be when a split opened up in the seam and leaked feathers.

It was three months of this, twelve hours at a stretch, before he met the three white men from the logging camp, Jameson, Fox and McNeil.

Fox would come in from the camps in the evenings and order a single ginger beer, which he sipped in the aisles with a thumb in his belt, perusing Hustler, Perfect 10. They mostly came sheathed in prohibitive sleeves but he always made noise over begging one open. He liked to see the pie, he said, before shelling out for a ten-dollar glossy. And one day, above the centerfold, through the strength of the glare off the airbrushed anatomy, Fox had asked William his name, his age and who his people were in town.

William Shaw. Nineteen, he said. And so long as you're asking, my Grandma is Cherokee.

Still around?

She's dead, said William.

So your grandma was Cherokee. *Was,* said Fox.

Fox soon came around with Jameson and McNeil and the three of them fast became regulars there. The other two men preferred Schiltz from the cooler and zip-lock parcels of beef-jerky, but Fox always drank the ginger beer and would sometimes treat himself to Skittles. A noxious combination of sours, William thought, though it seemed to suit this man just fine. Jameson was quiet, turkey-jowled, overweight, McNeil short and lean, with a faint Irish mouth. Fox towered over McNeil, with dark hair, and he might've been suave under very soft light had his face not looked so hard of sleep. As if a terror or a fetish or some mixture thereof distracted his head from the pillow most nights.

He would say, Hey, McNeil, and McNeil would say, What? and Fox would say, Listen. What's brown with black edges? and McNeil would posit, chuckling, Hmmm. A toasted piece of shit? And Fox would answer, No cigar. It's an Injun…he snarfled…who thinks that he's Elvis. And they all had a laugh orchestrated at William but not without grinning in his general direction. Then Fox would feint a rope-a-dope of punches at his stomach and McNeil, a guest-star in the Best of Fox Live, would throw in a couple hey-yo's for effect while Jameson sat there on his stool like an enormous and malcontent frog. William remained as stiff as birch, his fingers splayed open so wide on the counter you could've danced a knife between them.

One day Fox drew him aside. Jameson, McNeil and himself, he said, were fond of hunting out-of–season. Would William Shaw, descendent of chiefs, condescend to join them?

William had answered, I once killed a moose.

You mean a calf?

His head shook. A sight bigger than that.

Fox's eyes went thin with doubt. He drummed his fingers on the counter.

I caught it up in a trap that I'd laid in the leaves and I busted its head with a rock, said William.

Bullshit, you didn't.

I did.

Bullshit. I'll bet it was already wounded, said Fox.

William arranged some brochures on the counter.

Just say for a minute I killed it myself. What would you say to that? he said.

I'd say you shit luck and then piss it to match. He slapped William hard on the back.

And so, one week later, with a thirty of Schlitz and the white men outfitted in camo and flannel, the party had stood at the edge of the woods, plugging their Big-5-bought rifles with shells. It was a chilly Sunday that foretold of huge rain. All that week it had been raining. Most everyone else in the town was at church except these godless, kinless three, though William had heard Jameson had a wife who was not hard to look at. Fox and McNeil, however, were feral; there was no telling, even, how long they'd been friends. They might have met ten years ago or just last week picking over their lunches. Such was the glancing and chummy sadism that bided just beneath their talk, the mark of two men who had no real investment in what the other said or did.

The hunters debated among themselves which of them should go which way. William, in the know, stood apart from the three of them. He wore a look of scornful pity. Then William noticed that Fox was looking at him as if he'd done something astounding—played Lynyrd Skynyrd with his underarm, maybe, or pissed his name in perfect cursive.

Fox said, Where's your piece?

I don't use one, said William.

Don't carry a piece? said McNeil, snorting laughter. Hear that, Fox? He's above it.

You can't bag much of a deer with no rifle. Even Jameson here knows that, said Fox, and Jameson's head commenced to nod, his neck bunching up beneath his chin like a fleshy accordion bellows.

Well, I don't believe in guns.

Why not?

Cause they're an abomination, said William.

What's that? said McNeil. Didn't hear you. A what?

Abomination, William said. A flouting of the sacred hunt.

And what in damnation is that supposed to mean? Injuns use rifles the same as white men.

Not for sport, we don't, said William. We eat what we catch, A-Bolt or no.

You're hunting with the wrong three compadres then, son. Fox eyed him soberly, but not without interest. If you're coming with us just to teach us a lesson, then I'd advise you to turn back now.

You go in the footprints of your folk, he said, and I'll go in the footprints of mine.

Fox looked at William, sidelong at McNeil and then back at William again. He shrugged. Fair enough. The brave has spoken.

McNeil ululated then broke down laughing.

But don't you come whining to me later on when you haven't killed more than a woodchuck, said Fox.

With plans to meet around sunset at an old duckblind three miles upriver, the four of them entered the woods together in a sweeper's formation ranged William to Fox, but soon fanned out into different directions, hoping it would give them stealth. Fox went north, McNeil northeast and the brush-flattening vastness of Jameson west, so that William was left with no other course but to set his sights due east. The sky was a chilly claustrophobia of clouds, the ground unsure with forming mud. He picked his way down to a freshwater stream where he prepared to wince at gunfire with his fingers in the shallows. But none came. He perked up, heard a splashing nearby. And then he heard nothing for ceaselessly long. He sat there for what seemed like hours but what was only twenty minutes, and he started to suffer, as if for the first time, a wild confinement in his soul. A vast and disconsolate boredom set in, but also a sort of imprudent excitement. He felt that any second now some romantic disaster was sure to befall him. And then he heard the splash again. Knowing the trout were south, he turned. An albino deer with small pink eyes had stalled on its way across the stream and regarded him, its head craned round, with a look of high suspicion. It was powerful above the neck, but distinctly urchin-like along the ribs and in the legs. Hooving the rocks, it gave a snort. William got a little closer. But then, sensing something, which might've been him or a creature of even greater hazard, its muzzle swung bankward, then downstream again, after which it took off running. William fought only a brief indecision before he took off in pursuit.

The current grew stronger the farther they ran until the water was surging around William's calves. He saw that the deer had a hitch in its stride and its head swung loosely on its neck like a badly managed puppet. He was greatly enjoying the work of the chase, fleeter of foot with every step. There was maybe a hundred feet between them. Something up ahead smelled wrong. Then, at once, the deer stopped running, though for fear or exhaustion he knew not which. The wrongness he smelled, which was bracing and mineral, translated itself to a sound in his ears—a voided, vast and constant sound a thousand times his own capacity, driving itself through the veil of the air, resonant of doom. The animal seemed to sense it, too, and began to trot sidewise along with the current as if undecided which way it should turn. He realized there must be a falls up ahead and that if he could stay the deer's course downstream while hedging it in either side from the bank he might yet have the kind of kill that he'd been trying for. He imagined the faces of Fox Inc. when he brought them to a bloodless altar and must recount the chase for them, which he would do in lofty style. But the animal was clearly lame and much too scared to mind its neck; he would have to flush it far enough that the pull of the current became irresistible.

He began to creep toward it across the slick rocks with his center of gravity low to the water. In what seemed like a moment of dread comprehension, the deer snuffled once, twitched its ears, hung its head and approached where the land fell away at a trot. At the vanishing point it craned around while its hooves skidded helplessly over the stones and its small pink eyes met William's big brown ones just as its forelegs cleared the ledge. It was suspended at the drop-off for tense, amazing moment, like a snapshot of wildlife affixed to the air, but just as soon vanished out of sight in a scramble of legs and rolling muscle. William watched it thrash and turn until it integrated with the rapids.

He picked his way along the falls. The slope was wet and fraught with stones. West of him, the water roared with a sound so immense that he felt trapped inside it. When he got to the bottom, the deer was nowhere. The water rushed and flowed away. He scanned the clifftops east and west for signs of the three other men in his company, but all he saw were shrubs and birds, beyond them trees and clouds. He hunted in the water on his knees, getting soaked, clawing away the rocks and cursing. At last he dove and found himself in a gloomy world of roots and mud, but could keep his eyes open for only so long because of the drifting silt. He came up. The river was broad with no one on it. He was wet in the chill of afternoon. He thought it was fitting to yell in frustration, but all that he felt was a low, cheated sadness. An endless migration of carp went by, frisking about his ankles.

What was left of the day he spent hunting the deer out along the high cliffs, and among the steep shoals, and upon the rock isles in the cliff's overhang, as if distance, depth or darkness were enough to conceal a creature so lovely and peerless as that one. But his search was no more than a matter of course. He'd known all along that he'd happen on nothing. The snapshot of the deer hovering beyond the cliff with its pink eyes entreating the land to be under it had crystallized in William's mind as one orchestrated and intended for him. He found a rifle casing near the edge of the cliff adjacent to the one that the deer had leapt off, but there were no attendant footprints in the loose dirt there and no way of knowing if the casing was recent or ejected a long time ago in that place. Until nightfall called him back to the duckblind, he crossed and re-crossed the narrow rapids, crouched in the shadows of grottoes and inlets, knelt at the edges of nearby cliffs with an imaginary rifle angled down above the water. The physical geometry of his failure made no sense to him at all.

145

When he got to the duckblind, a storm had kicked up. It was a freak autumn storm and it rained itself prodigiously, driving across the land in sheets. He poked his head into the room and first saw only Jameson, who overflowed a wooden chair with his big Golem's hands folded neatly before him.

Heyer, he said. His voice was soft.

Hey yourself, said William. Rain.

The logs in the wall were unevenly spaced and water from the storm was everywhere.

If it ain't Pocahontas, said McNeil from the shadows, jackknifed unsteadily back in his chair.

The chair-legs complained as he leaned from the darkness. Any luck out there today?

A little, said William, coming into the room. I saw a white deer. An albino, I think. I chased her over the falls.

You what? said McNeil, with a twisted smile. Chased her from the falls, you say? Now I'm not saying I'm an expert but don't a man keep what he kills most-times?

I looked everywhere, said William. Nowhere to be found.

Well doesn't that beat all, said McNeil. A certified Albino deer. You say you couldn't find her, huh? Maybe she was hid in the water.

If she was sunk I would've found her. The water there wasn't so deep, said William.

But you said she was white, *all white*, like a ghost.

I'm not making it up, said William. The hell with you—where's Fox?

Taking his ease somewheres, I suppose

The gaps between the logs lit up a fierce white. A few seconds later, thunder spoke. McNeil went wobbling in his chair and even the fat man jumped a little.

God save him if he's out in that. McNeil betrayed a weary sympathy.

Amen, said the fat man, eyes casting about him, apparently sorry that he'd spoken.

They began to hear hollers not far from the doorway, feebly at first beneath the wind. A small churning figure emerged from the rain and labored uphill in a crouch towards the duckblind, stopping betimes to shift its weight and readjust its course. The thunder and the rain increased. They could not hear the words it hollered. And then William saw that it was Fox, but humped with a dark unwieldy shape.

He shouted, Look here. Look here what I found. It'll make me rich, by God.

The men disbanded from the door to give him floor-space to maneuver, and he called out a space on the boards, which they made, pushing the chairs and the stools to the wall and removing the thirty of Schlitz from the crate. He dropped the white deer with a slap to the floor, went high-stepping over its flank to survey. William had known that Fox would have it the moment he'd seen him approaching uphill. He briefly laid eyes on a dark ragged wound that had found out the base of the animal's neck and then another in its skull, but Fox stepped in front of him, blocking his view, and stomped off the mud from his boots.

Sniped the bitch. He caught his breath. She's a son of a bitch of a thing, isn't she?

He bent over gasping, and picked out a chair, and sitting down in it he heaved there in silence.

I was up on those bluffs—hey McNeil, ginger beer me.

Here go, said McNeil, hand lost in the cooler.

Like I said, he went on. I was up on those bluffs and I saw this deer just standing there. Not a care in the world, this pure white deer. Got spooked at the edge of the falls, I guess. He drank interminably of his beer and exhaled. So I took aim and shot her down. Put one in her dome to make sure when I found her.

McNeil wore a titled uncomfortable smile. Why she could be a unicorn.

I don't see a horn, do you? Unicorn my ass, said Fox.

The Irishman crumpled his beer, wiped his mouth. The smiled had withered on his face. Reckon Fox here caught you out in a lie.

Fox looked up through dripping hair.

What lies you been telling there, William? he said.

Then the deer began to thrash, or so William assumed at first, so uncanny and quick and insane was the movement, like a trophy deer trying to wrench from its mounting. But really it just twitched with vigor, laboring under a compromised spine, trying to leverage its wrecked upper-half towards where the rain was blowing through the duckblind's open door. A thin drool of blood came away from its tongue, collected and webbed on its face. McNeil gaped. The mewling power had escaped it; its animal breath came sick and heavy. None of the men knew how to react to this pitiful circus in front of them. What William could not understand was how the deer was still alive, how it could be shot in the head and still struggle like something vengeful and aggrieved.

Punch her card another time. McNeil popped a Schlitz and drew foam off the ridges.

Nah, said Fox. I had my shot. But I'll let someone else take a crack if he's game. Hey, he said. And turned to William. Indulge me a sec with this thing.

Mechanically, William's arm reached out and when it came back he could feel the wet metal. He then realized that the challenge still stood—had been hanging about for a minute at least.

He won't do it, said McNeil. Play that fucker through yourself.

You won't? said Fox.

William studied the gun.

You really, really won't? he said.

The deer started to move again but could not execute the impulse. Its head was more strange on its neck than before. There were membranes of blood in its eyes and it gasped.

Now, this is pathetic, said McNeil in chagrin. Jameson, fork that bad boy over.

But Jameson, who held his gun and stood a bit apart from them, had been shaking his head at the pitiable thing for longer than any man there had been party.

He said something then.

McNeil said, What?

What? said Fox.

But Jameson did not answer.

He was already busy with the rifle, tending to its bolts and knobs.

If you're going to do that, mind the safety.

Skeptical teeth in the fat man's direction, courtesy of Fox.

He took the suggestion. Then he aimed. The deer lay as flat as a sheet on the boards. William's eyes ticked man to man. The time to do something was now, absolutely.

Jameson fired. The deer's face flew apart, the water on the walls ran red and William was looking, not down at the killing, but at Jameson's soft, mounded head from the side, and he was looking at it, also, from a curious angle, as though along a sort of plane, which he soon realized was the scope of the rifle that Fox had never taken from him. The safety was gone, the muzzle fixed. William Shaw was aiming at another human being. He lowered the rifle quickly, shaking, thumbed the safety back to safe.

Pretty close, said Fox. Woo-wee. I'll tell you, that was pr*eee*ty close.

Everyone there was fixed dumbly on Jameson, the rifle smoking in his hands.

For everyone, save Jameson, had seen the angle of the gun—and yet, for a minute, or more than a minute, no one told him, no one spoke, allowing the fat man to rest in his innocence, to enjoy the faint smile gathering on his face. He shouldered the rifle and knelt towards the deer, awkwardly, slowly, the big rifle dangling, until he was leaning above the wrecked void of what had been the creature's muzzle, most of it blasted away, save the eye, which was perched on a sort of escarpment of bone. And as the fat man knelt in closer, his belly and knees creasing tenderly, vastly, the brave imagined in that eye that Jameson could see them all, like a group cameo of some old hunting party where William's white pappy had bagged him a raghorn.

But he wanted the fat man to look up and see him, for Jameson to turn his way, as if to confirm in his own mind, at least, the unspeakable shame of what he'd done.

King Dodd

Dodd was an orphan and a baker of bread. He looked like Dodd, walked like Dodd, smelled like Dodd and talked like Dodd. He exemplified Dodd-ness to such a degree he could only be Dodd and no one else; and yet, at the same time, he could've been anyone, for there existed a disjunction between his body and his mind that to him, on the worst days, seemed black and unfixable. While Dodd's mind was a scramble of dreams, desires, memories, Dodd's physical presence—precisely, his face—was no more than matter that called itself Dodd. And though he moved through time and space in a tireless accord with his humanoid functions, like walking and talking and smelling, etcetera, Dodd was not perceived by others as a person should be, as you are perceiving these words right now, as you yourself can be perceived, provided you're not Dodd. He didn't take pains to hide himself, but walked upright, chest out, chin buoyant and projected his voice when he spoke, like a thespian. And yet there was nothing in Dodd that was freakish, not outwardly freakish, at least, like a hump, and this, perhaps, was Dodd's true curse, that he should appear quintessentially average, and so much so, in fact, that Dodd was so much more the freak. And no one could speak of Dodd's eyes, or Dodd's hair, or Dodd's face, or Dodd's build, or Dodd's clothes, or Dodd's posture, for no one had the proper words for a series of traits so aggressively bland.

Dodd was a being allergic to sense. He didn't show up on the radars of others.

If you placed him in a concrete room, and watched him through a two-way mirror, then the room that contained him would pour into Dodd or, depending on your outlook, Dodd would pour into the room. He would turn the same color as the walls, an ashen hue and you would wonder how it was you picked him out of a crowd and brought him to that room to begin with.

Wherever Dodd was, he was not.

But Dodd was an orphan and a baker of bread, two facts, be it known, that made Dodd Dodd in a world that might sooner have let him be no one. Dodd's orphan status could be proven on paper, specifically, the documents from Dodd's orphanage that included but were not strictly limited to the filed-away notice announcing him: Dodd. Dodd's mother and father, whoever they were, had given Dodd up for adoption post-partum, and whether a matter of youth or slim means—Dodd's parents were young and quite poor when they had him—or whether Dodd, in appearance, was too much of a cipher for any young couple to sire and protect with the necessary quota of love and affection due every child, including Dodd, no one can ever know for sure. Dodd was ugly and unlovable but invisibly so, in the way of the dead or a faraway war, and anyone keen to the features of others, namely Dodd's parents, whomever they were, would recoil from Dodd's presence without ever knowing what it was they were recoiling from. Dodd was an aura, a breeze, a shade, an effigy of a man named Dodd. In the Brooklyn ward where Dodd was born, in the orphanage cot where he sweated through boyhood and later in a bigger cot in the one-room apartment where Dodd had washed up, he accepted the pallor of his sheets and became something squeezed from a tube, a pale blob. It is little cause for wonder he could never be loved and even less so that he lived all alone. Dodd's parents, then, felt exempt from blame, for how could a child as scarce as Dodd be abandoned with the same heartlessness as a real one?

Outside of the papers attesting to Dodd—that were not, by the way, in Dodd's possession—the only other evidence of Dodd in the world was the job that he held as a baker of bread at Pan de Amor in Sunset Park, Brooklyn. Dodd would rise early and do Dodd's ablutions, doddering, Dodd-like, in front of the mirror. He stared at himself and he said the word Dodd and he blinked like a mole in the halogen light. Then he would dress for a fiber-rich breakfast, oatmeal with bananas, which he ate on his bed, and after would slowly smoke one Winston Red in the chair below his single window, watching the smoke as it curled in the light and broke against his Dodd-like body. On getting to work he would sign the timesheet and perhaps say a word to his boss, Manuel, who consistently failed to notice Dodd and had even withheld a couple paychecks because of it. His greeting unheard—and he wondered, then, spoken?—Dodd continued through the kitchen to the counter in the back, and there would lose himself for hours to the piston-like plunge, knead and roll of his work. When lunchtime came then Dodd would eat, if only to prove he was fit to house something even if it was just food. He ate loudly, voraciously, but without real pleasure. The presence of his coworkers depleted his appetite. The oatmeal with bananas he ate in the morning was in truth the only meal that he ever enjoyed because he could eat it alone. When there were others around, as there were at Dodd's work, Dodd's need to convince them of his corporeality was far too insistent to share space with eating; and so Dodd would lunch rudely, with weird epic slurps, commending the taste of his savorless food, especially when it displeased him. His coworkers went about their business, stepping over Dodd's legs where he sat on an egg-crate, taking his haunted, Dodd-like lunch. And since the egg-crate was positioned most days against the steel flank of the dough-rolling counter, the metal would give Dodd a decorative look, as if he'd been dipped in a bath of hot silver.

When Dodd arrived home he didn't leave his apartment until the next day when he went in to work. He sketched through the night at a desk in his room, a drafting desk he'd bought with his accumulated savings, and worked with fine pens from the art-supply store, each inscribed with the name of a laudable artist. And since his rent was fairly cheap, his acquaintances none, and his intake just middling, Dodd was content to indulge his one hobby even if it was only Dodd. For it was Dodd who sketched Dodd at Dodd's prized drafting desk, Dodd who watched Dodd until Dodd's eyes were bleary, Dodd who probed Dodd for the sly inner-life that artists seek out in their subjects. And when Dodd drew himself, Dodd would do it from memory, on the basis of Dodd knowing Dodd to a T. The completed self-portraits and aborted ones—both—Dodd kept amidst the shuffle of his battered black portfolio, but now and again Dodd would leaf through the sheets, complimenting himself on the ones that rang true: You look very handsome in this one, Dodd. You almost look real enough to blink.

When Dodd wasn't at home, he walked the streets, the more populated by humans the better. In Manhattan it was Times Square, Union Square, Columbus Circle, Lincoln Center, Penn Station, Wall Street, Chinatown; in Brooklyn Seventh Avenue, Borough Hall, Fulton Mall; in Queens Queensboro Plaza and certain parts of Jackson Heights. He would go into frequented shops, if they drew him, but oftener would stand outside, watching himself in both bright and dull glass as the roil of pedestrians hid and revealed him to good, self-affirming effect. In the parks Dodd was green, in the trains orange-black, on the sidewalks a sort of mélange, a dull grey. Near traffic his voice was the honking of horns, in an open-air market the calls of food vendors, in Coney Island, on the beach, the crying of gulls and the buffet of waves on the sand. Close enough to Dodd to smell him—and this, of course, was very rare—he exuded a sort of big-city miasma: hotdogs, exhaust, treated sewage and rain.

Moving through the subway tunnels, in the cross-ambulation of stations and streets, he walked always against the daytime crowd at a speed that was reckless by most city standards. He veered too close to passersby and tried to catch their eyes but couldn't and Dodd quickly learned, with a mild resignation, to savor the breezes their bodies gave off. He retreated in these moments into scientific principles, the simple, cold comfort of A passing B. He'd been lonely for so long that he felt himself beyond it, like a fading constellation at the end of all time.

One day, however, Dodd's fortune changed. It was a Tuesday in the summer and he'd gone to Coney Island, his favorite destination in the city year round. The barkers called to everyone—even and especially him—and the raggedy beach mutts would follow sometimes, chasing smells that were not Dodd's. With the salt on his skin, and the sand in his hair, and the taste of a funnel cake crisp on his tongue—funnel cake that Dodd ate free when the vendor had failed to notice Dodd and the next man in line had walked off prematurely after placing an order for Dodd's favorite treat—he waited on the N train steps as the people emerged in the cottony heat. Last among them came a giant—a crooked, loping seven-footer towering above the dark; and covering his face entire save a hole on the left where the eye stared out whitely, a purple destruction of veins and skin cells, the afterimage of a caul. When the man gained the top of the steps he saw Dodd, which is to say he looked right at him—but he'd never been looked at so frankly before, and with such certainty on the part of the looker. It made his blood reverse its course and made his tender stomach plunge. The man watched Dodd until he'd passed, or rather peered down on account of his height and Dodd saw his birthmark was slightly upraised like poisonous braille on a rainforest frog. Dodd spun around and he called out, You there. But the tall man had already walked into traffic. He stood on the median, hands at his sides, with the oncoming cars going by him and by him. Dodd ventured out with a frail, reaching motion but was nearly side-clipped by a series of cars. By the time the light had changed and he was able to cross, the man had gained the sidewalk on the opposite side.

Dodd didn't draw himself that night. Instead he drew the birthmarked man in the moment he'd seemed to see Dodd on the steps. He drew the almost imperceptible widening of his eyes, the curious chink of his mouth, the flexed nostrils. Dodd conceived of twenty drafts, a good many decent but wide of the mark. And slept maybe an hour or two, leaving ink trails in the sheets when he tossed. The face had so possessed him that it tracked behind his eyes and fevered what few dreams he had before morning.

Dodd's next day off was Saturday. He'd been planning to tour the west-side piers, but yesterday's encounter called for something extreme, a complete redirection of his energies. So, instead of Dodd boarding the Manhattan-bound train, he boarded the line headed deeper into Brooklyn, and rode it south to Bensonhurst to the orphanage where he'd been raised—or the institution, rather, he'd been permitted to exist in—which not only still stood but was still operational, with a crop of drab boys coming in every month. Dodd walked down the tree-lined blocks to the scrolled ironwork of Sacred Heart and sat on a promising species of bench at the empty bus-stop across the street. Today was the day, Dodd told himself, that Dodd would furnish evidence of Dodd on paper. Any minute he would rise, stroll up to the door and knock his hardest with the knocker; then, once inside, at the wire-mesh of the record room, he would state his name, Dodd, and be served by the clerk. But the bus growled past, the sun charged down, the orphans and nuns came and went up the steps. Every so often Dodd rose from the bench, but just as soon sat when his legs jellied under him.

Around three o' clock, or so Dodd assumed—watchless, he measured the day by the heat—a diminutive man all in black with a briefcase approached from the direction of the subway. He was not just remarkable for his stature, which a block away appeared, clinically, to be a dwarf's, but also how he walked along, a brisk, proto-shuffle, his arms at his sides. But it was only when he halted at the base of the steps to open his briefcase and peer inside that Dodd saw the man was bereft of a neck. The collar peeking from his suit was all but a wedge between chin and brief shoulders, and his head, Dodd imagined, if you twisted it right, might have come off like an action doll's. When the man was assured of his briefcase's contents, he locked the hasp and rushed inside.

In fifteen minutes, Dodd was ready. He rose from the bench and took a step, which was followed—praise Dodd—by another one still, and scarcely was Dodd patting Dodd on the back on what must be a steady clip than he found himself standing, damp with sweat, in front of the orphanage doors. But Dodd's fists had staged a mutiny. Try as he might, they would not knock. And his predicament grew every second more pressing, for when he turned around again to send the bench a parting glance he saw advancing up the block, to the tempo of heels, a guardian of the state with her ward at her side. At which Dodd regressed to an earlier Dodd, the hand of a stranger enmeshed with Dodd's hand—the hands of strangers hot and cold, and damp and dry, and weak and strong, escorting Dodd hither and thither through time, to the tempos of heels, and of flats, and of wingtips. Dodd turned around and, for once in his life, willed himself into the wood-grain. But the door opened out in a rush of cold air, forcing Dodd down a step or two, and revealing the man in the suit with no neck. He stood a bit far of the gloom of the lobby, but short of the dazzle of the stairs, and he clenched his briefcase at his chest in a tense and both-handed, reptilian grip, as if whatever he had in it must be guarded at all costs. He looked into Dodd's eyes with such unflinching intensity that he might've been looking entirely past him, and Dodd turned around to be confronted by the twosome. Dodd had thought to notice them, especially the little ward, with the logic that to do so would be to take steps along a healthy plane of thinking. But Dodd did not have time for both; it was either the man with no neck, or the boy.

The little boy gaped at the man, but not Dodd, while the woman averted her face for politeness.

When the doors of the orphanage had shut, the man with no neck asked Dodd for the time. His voice was as lisping and soft as a snake's—the voice of a snake in a children's cartoon. Dodd looked at his watchless wrist and then the summer sky.

Three thirty, he said. Maybe quarter of four.

The man's head bobbed. Thank you, he said.

Up close his eyes were shiny and opaque as black buttons, his nose so hooked it was almost a spiral. He wore creased black trousers, matching blazer, clip-on tie, azure dress-shirt, and on top of it all sat the ill-fitting collar, which housed in its wallow a small, round head.

He fixed upon Dodd with a tense, eager look and Dodd fixed him back through the fog of old solitude. But before Dodd could take his arm or ask what he was doing there, the neckless man nodded and light-footed off without even so much as a lisp of farewell. Dodd stood for a time at the top of the steps, vibrating with the summons of the man's sudden greeting. When his molecules had gathered to the point where he could follow, the neckless man was crossing the street a block south.

Dodd made up the distance at an enterprising lope. But the neckless man was still ahead. A pack of schoolchildren, effervescent with dismissal, parted for Dodd like a dog or a breeze, and Dodd was caught amidst their bubbling before he tore free and went on. The man turned down the subway steps—a gnome into its mountain-keep. Descending himself, Dodd was caught in the draft of the train coming into the station below him; and when he finally did arrive, after mashing his token, not fitting the slot, the man had made the outbound train, or shuttled like a rat into the reaches of the tunnel.

Dodd rode the trains for the rest of the day in hopes that he'd spot the man again. In the vicinity of Kensington, near Courtelyou Road, Dodd thought he saw the man on the Manhattan-bound side, but upon looking closer it was just a Hasid, as tall as the man and dark-suited as him—and yet nothing so much as a boy in a shawl with a slight, unmistakable neck.

When the N crested out past the Queensboro Bridge it came to Dodd that night had fallen. He dropped off to sleep suddenly in his seat. When the train got to Ditmars, the conductor came on to announce that it was going out of service and a subwayman went down the cars to flush the laggard riders. The man to Dodd's left, a bedraggled day-drunk still rumpled in his suit from work, was just as asleep as Dodd was, if not more; the subwayman woke only him. Dodd came to in a Yonkers train yard, slumped in the dark of the car.

The next day Dodd called out of work and rode every line in the four-borough system. He saw neither the man with the blighted face nor the neckless man of yesterday, though he thought he saw them both several times and together, the giant and his gnome. That night at his house he drew one, then the other. A fever of portraits amassed on his desk. When his efforts to capture them separately failed, Dodd began to draw the men in many different combinations; he drew them back to back, hands clasped, sometimes inserting himself for good measure. In Dodd's work, they were a threesome, a family almost. Dodd figured himself as the child every time.

Toward dawn Dodd awoke to a rustling outside. A woman was rummaging through his trash. Though the woman was black, her skin's pigment was spotty. Her arms and her shoulders, the v of her neck, which the dirty blue dress she was wearing revealed, were dabbed pink in parts, like an ill-conceived dye-job. She was looking up and down the street with a half-confused, half-furtive air, and her frizzy black hair, also stripped of some pigment, wafted across her face like ash.She inspected each item she pulled from the trash as if it posed some hidden meaning: empty bags of Instant Oatmeal, and empty packs of Winston Reds, dental floss, banana peels, a dishtowel stiff with ink; and she came on, progressively, large wads of paper that she gently dissected and peeked inside. Finding something or nothing at the centers of the wads, she would balance them close in the crook of her arm or throw them back into the trash until there were eight in a perfect succession between her gaunt wrist and her elbow. Though Dodd usually saved every drawing he did so he could learn from past mistakes, the ones that he'd done of the men from the trains—many of which, if not all, were false starts—had proven too much of a thwartedness to him to look at more than once or twice. He'd thrown them out the night before, suddenly bitter and sick at the sight of them. Now the woman drew them wide and snapped them taut to chase the wrinkles. She held them out in front of her and peered at them from different angles, before deciding on two, which she folded into one and placed in a kangaroo-pocket on her dress; then she recrumpled an unneeded six and gave them to the trash again. Turning away, her frizzed hair caught an updraft. One mottled cheek flashed at Dodd in the sun.

For the three days that followed Dodd kept to a diet of drawing the men and then riding the trains. He slept three hours a night at most and ate twitching meals in the dark of his kitchen: bananas and bread-balls and glasses of milk. And yet he felt a waxing in his powers of perception, a strange heightening of his sense of himself as one who received, discerned, collected. The screeching of the subway's brakes would make his thoughts disperse like birds; the car's slightest jolt made him jump from his seat; the chatter of others stormed his brain like a globe in a science museum. The people themselves were holograms, transgressing their outlines, projecting out at him. A few times he even cried out in alarm when the doors opened up to admit them.

On the fourth day Dodd lived in a porous enclosure; the world filtered in and it churned around Dodd. The door at the end of his car shuttled open and a curious figure came in through the coupling. The man had dark skin and was covered in rags, a patchwork of cloth, nylon and wool. He hobbled along on a rude wooden cane with a bucket of alms chiming dull at his side and wore a battered cardboard sign that looked to be pasted with newsprint. People down the train-car dropped change in the bucket without looking up from their laps. His face was no face, but the ruins of one, a haphazard network of holes and scar tissue. His eyes were gone, his cheek flapped open and his mouth fluttered raggedly back from his teeth. On the sign was a feature from the Post—Lab Technician Scarred with Acid—and below the text a photo of the man before the accident. He was middle-aged, black, with a close shaven head. The picture from the paper had him smiling, lab-coated, surrounded by beakers and chemical courses, toasting the shot with a vial of some fluid. The lab technician stopped near Dodd and shook the bucket in his face. Quarters, he said, are a notch in your belt. The man upstairs is keeping track. Dodd dug in his pockets and fished out change, which he dropped with a nod in the bucket. Dodd waited until he'd reached the door and then he rose to follow.

The man made a sweep of the train, end to end, and then at the last car turned back for another. Dodd shadowed him like a diligent

159

footman, stopping when he stooped for change and hobbling along in his wake. The people looked down as they passed, swallowed hard or stared at him without compunction. Sometimes their eyes passed over Dodd and the novelty of this tickled him. They transferred—the F to the Q to the 7—and they panhandled down the whole length of the cars. After a few unbroken hours, they transferred from the L train to the G at Metropolitan. In a riderless car the man sat down. Dodd sat down across from him and peered at him closely, transfixed by where his skull showed through. The man sat up straight, his knees drawn together, the bucket of alms balancing in his lap.

The man detrained at Classon Avenue. Climbing behind his flattened shanks and the deep prophecy of the sound of his cane, Dodd cast an eye on the train as it left him, breaking and jewelling to switch at the junction. They emerged into sunlight, pursuer, pursued, though Dodd had reconsidered who was who many times. They passed through games of foursquare, young men trading rhymes, gossiping flocks of wide-hipped women who hushed at the sight of the man's death's head before recommencing their talk. Dodd turned the shade of the crumbling walls, the weeds growing up through the sidewalk. The people grew fewer, the walls fell away, and soon they were walking through whole carless lots where the garbage was heaped in monoliths. And then, at the end of a long boarded block that did not continue but met with another, forming a three-sided stop at the confluence, a tall and bright yet motley building chunked above the dark horizon. From a distance it resembled a church, but less austere; it reached four stories high in the tenement-style before erupting at its summit in a mess of outcroppings knocked together out of wood and wire and glass. The building's rooftop—or its gabling, more like—was a headache of reflective planes: shattered mirror, torn tin roofing, oddments of Lucite and metal and quartz. At the bottom of the building was a simple black door. Here the man stopped, turned around.

You there, he said. Don't *we* know each other?

I'm not sure. We might, said Dodd.

All of us know you, he said. And whether or not you're aware, you know us.

Who's *we?*

Why, *us,* said the man with no face. We've *always* been waiting for you. You're Dodd.

The man knocked once. They waited some. The man knocked again and they waited some more. A mustering of locks could be heard beyond the door; Dodd counted four pins slipping free as it opened. The inside was gloomy, infested with dust and it took Dodd a while to recognize the man who'd answered. He cut the same imposing figure as when Dodd had first seen him, but now he wore something akin to a smile. Behind him, in the dress, was the woman with the skin. He saw their hands were slightly touching. They watched him intently, expecting some comment and when he smiled weakly said, Dodd, in a chorus. The man swept an arm toward the gloaming behind him, stepped back from the door.

The interior of the building had a curious design, if design it could even be said to have. Half-destroyed walls ran slant through the rooms and the floor was a sea of loose brick, chunks of plaster, jagged suggestions of metal and wood. The rooms didn't so much attest to half-completion as they did to the fulfillment of some prophesied collapse and as Dodd and the faceless man passed through by the slow stumping sound of the faceless man's cane, Dodd was suddenly conscious of indistinct figures that wove among the ruined walls. At first they were no more than rumors of matter, shadows crisscrossing through far deeper dark, and only when they had achieved the room's center, where a fat cone of light titled down from above, did Dodd perceive the figures for the prodigies they were. A child with a hairlip skipped past Dodd, swinging a big coil of wire like a mace. An old woman in rags went wandering by who at first appeared to have no defects, but as she passed under the light's far edge Dodd saw a long and a calcified horn that curved, like sagged wax, from a brow mild with age. A man with ripely swollen legs; a girl with goiters at her ears; a skinny blonde woman with dark scoops for eyes, her face engulfed whole and grotesque by psoriasis. They all gazed at Dodd, moved about him like supplicants. Some of them ventured a curtsy or bow before falling back into darkness.

Before long the man halted in front of a ladder that had been bolted to the structure of a crumbling wall. Dodd gazed up its many rungs and saw they stretched clear to the top of the ceiling. Looking closer, he saw there were no floors to speak of, just shallow alcoves that were spanned by the ladders. The alcoves were twinned on the western side where yet another ladder made a similar ascent, and the higher Dodd looked the more ladders there were, ladders running parallel and crosswise and slant, a network of ladders dividing the murk into pockets of empty air. An improvised skylight was rent in the ceiling, and through it Dodd saw shards of blue, a few skittish clouds passing on.

Climb, said the man. Your rooms await.

Climb? said Dodd. My rooms? How high?

But the faceless man had walked away.

And so Dodd started climbing, unwilling at first, fighting a dark urge to look down. The alcoves before him were recessed and dim and yet he could make out the rumpling of bedding, the indistinct outlines of tables and chairs. Every so often a humanoid form would creep to the edge and observe him unseen, yet whenever he stopped they crept back on all fours and were lost to the darkness like beetles. And Dodd saw the endless crosshatching of ladders was only one of several methods of conveyance to the top: guy-ropes and pulleys and zip-lines spanned taut, and lengths of chain swayed like industrial vines, and plastic nubs and grooved hand-holds were staggered up and down the walls. Filigreed droplets came down through the ceiling from a sun-shower, maybe, or some sort of leak, and Dodd's ascent became a parallax of ladders and chains and small, slanted rain down a tunnel of light. Dodd was struck by the sensation of moving up and down at once. As he might've predicted, imbalance set in.

And here, at the top of the ladder Dodd climbed, was an alcove more spacious than all of the others, bathed in a sourceless and rose-colored lighting. Dodd paused; Dodd paused and Dodd did what Dodd mustn't, Dodd looked and the rubble went yawing beneath him. The faceless man was all but lost, a tiny, ineffectual spotter.

You shouldn't do that, said a voice to his right. You've got to get your sea-legs first.

The neckless man stood at the edge of the alcove.

What am I supposed to do now? said Dodd.

Come take a look at your room, said the man.

My room?

Yes, your room.

You mean, my *rooms*.

Whichever you like, he said. They're yours.

So Dodd squared himself with the lip of the alcove, stepped onto the wooden floor. The man stepped away with the same deference that the birthmarked and faceless men had shown. Inside was a cot, and a couch, and a table, and a kitchen-cum-pantry, and even a toilet. How had they gotten it up here? thought Dodd. How had they even installed working plumbing? But then he laid eyes on the half-finished portraits that the woman had taken from his trash. There was one at each end of the couch, spread apart, and then tamped down with volumes to level the creases. Next to the portraits a cream-colored folder, Dodd's name, in faint type, stickered onto the tab, and in the folder's upper corner, no bigger than a fly, the heart-and-shield sign of the orphanage. Sitting on the table was a new pad of paper and near it a packet of Dodd's favorite pens, and near the pens were Winston Reds, a single box, the wrap still on them. On top of the pack sat a slim, silver lighter.

The man with no neck was still there, next to Dodd, watching him peruse the room.

The penthouse suite, he said to Dodd. No home but the best for our Dodd.

And he grinned.

And Dodd felt for an instant, amidst the dim alcove, at the top of the frightening and endless ascent, in the church that was not quite a church but also not quite *not* one either, in this marginal place where the man with no face had guided Dodd and Dodd alone, and before that the neckless man, and before that the birthmarked one, and before that Dodd wondering about this moment, here, at last—Dodd felt that Dodd was finally Dodd in a way Dodd had never experienced before, and he saw that his Dodd-colored body was fleshy, a dotted outline shaded in, made firm and made real by the rose-colored light that flooded the chambers of Dodd's kingdom come.

But then he noticed something strange.

It was something about the room, its objects, each of them handpicked or salvaged for Dodd, and arrayed in a way that would cotton Dodd to them. And then Dodd saw it was the bed, or rather, strictly put, the cot; and not the cot itself, its shape, or where inside it was positioned, but rather that it had been made and made well, right down to the corners of the sheets, the high left of which had been tucked back, just slightly, to welcome the sleeper, i.e. Dodd—to lightly assure Dodd that even Dodd's slumber rested, now, in the kindest, most capable hands. It wasn't like a hotel cot. It wasn't like a cot at all. It was rather the deepest of human embellishments, and Dodd's stomach turned with revulsion to see it.

And Dodd knew then this was no home and that he, Dodd, could be no king.

For Dodd could lead no man nowhere, unless it were into that man's own negation. Unless it were into the innermost heart of all that Dodd wished for himself yet denied. Unless it were into the labyrinth of Dodd, which Dodd had seen so long in others, but which, for the first time, Dodd witnessed in Dodd, in his need to be gone from that place, in his unhappiness.

The Sub-Leaser

And so I returned from a series of errands to find my apartment unalterably changed. Which change, I should say, was in fact several changes that had, in collusion, effected the one by dint of a sly and concerted campaign against the state of my rooms preceding my absence. Rooms, and not room, to be clear on one thing; namely, that I, their primary tenant, was only fiscally and moreover physically liable for the sustained occupation of one, my room, while the other, which lay around a bend and down a splintered wooden hallway from my own, the north room, I had leased for undetermined months to a certain third party little known to me then. But more of him, the sub-leaser, the stranger, to come.

It is the matter of the change that I wish to embark on.

My apartment is a standard one for the part of the city where I live. It begins at the door, which opens, like so, to show the splintered wooden hallway that I mentioned before. On the right is a bathroom, ill-sequenced of tile, with a sink built onto the wall and a bathtub, where a thin and mildewed curtain hangs, clad in a pattern of green and white plaid. To the left of the curtain, an insolent toilet, coated with a film of brown. Above the toilet is a window of thick, smeary glass that peers out on a bend in a courtyard of stone which does not correspond, I have need to observe, to the crook of the L that makes up the apartment. Continuing down the splintered hall, tandem to the bathroom on the right, is a kitchen, with a wide metal sink, and a stovetop and oven, and copious shelf-space above, where sit foodstuffs. Facing the shelving, a circular table, unmatted and scarred, with extendable leaves. Though these leaves, I should mention, have not been extended for some inhospitable months by my calendar.

Roughly tandem to the kitchen is the room in which I take my rest. My room, the north room, leased only to me, is a large and ascetic, say, scholarly space, bisected along the western wall by a naked lead pipe grown outrageously hot in what are now, as I write this, the dog days of winter. Next to the pipe sits a modest bookshelf where I have invested a paperback library—philosophical texts by dead men with spry minds in whom I have vested a tentative trust. Northeast of the shelf, in the room's farthest corner, hunkers the whiteness of the bed, and next to the bed, a lacquered side-table, where a number of disparate items reside, including, but not always limited to, the book I happen to be reading, a flexible, prehensile lamp, a humidifier that severs the air with its shrill, unbending jet of steam, a glass of night-water with things floating in it whose molecular makeup I would rather not know, things native to here, to the pipes underneath, to the far reservoirs, kept by concrete, that do their best to keep me healthy.

There is nothing on the walls of the room where I sleep. The white of the paint there has proven acceptable.

Beyond the living room, in the back of the apartment, lies the south room, the strange room, the room not mine, and of which I prefer, on the whole, not to speak. For it marks what is clearly, in my mind at least, the origin of the greater change that I found had come over the whole of the rooms upon coming back from the series of errands. As if, like some malignancy, the change had begun in that room and spread outward. It had been occupied, the room, I mean, by the sub-leaser little known to me, who had come to inquire about said room after happening, he claimed, on an advertisement for it. That was the word he had used, the word *happen*—I happened on the ad, he'd said, while reading the paper this morning at breakfast. As if to say in truth that he'd done nothing of the sort, but had had the room in mind to sub-lease for some time, and this feigned indifference the ultimate ploy to ensure it would be his, and quick. When I returned from my day running errands he had gone, without a word in advance or a courtesy call, and the apartment without him was utterly changed, not because he had left but because he had been there.

However, he did leave a note, the sub-leaser, less a source of information than it was a kind of cipher, tamped beneath the grey saltshaker at the center of the table with extendable leaves. It was a word-processed note, as opposed to handwritten, which struck me as odd for a couple of reasons: 1. As a note, it did not merit printing, which was what had produced it, a printer, I mean, and not a typewriter, as might stand to reason, the latter machine on the whole more conducive to jotting a note on the fly, for quick viewing, and the former altogether best for composing a statement or even a missive, while the note, as you will find, was neither; 2. The sub-leaser, for whatever reason, had quit the south room with remarkable haste in the five-hour period I was gone, which was really four hours, by the sub-leaser's clock, for he would have been wise to account for, at least, a buffering margin of one or more hours between when he had fixed for himself to be gone, and roughly the time he expected me home, which was barely enough for the moving essentials, let alone to sit down at a laptop computer, format a note and print the note out; and 3. It consisted of the following words, which were odd irrespective of their method of production:

Hey,
Enclosed bills ($60) are for Tatiana, arriving 2/2/09. Thanks for the shelter, however brief. And good luck!
Sincerely,
Hank
P.S.—Tatiana's #: (212) 676-2398

Hank's *enclosed bills* were indeed in the note, congruent the seam of the folded up paper. They were not meant to count towards the rent, I knew, which he had always paid by check, and which he had paid me in full the day prior by way of said check slipped under my door, perhaps, I reflected, to avoid circumstances that would have been colored, on his part at least, by the awkward foreknowledge of his imminent departure, which he planned to effect the next day, i.e., this one. But then again, I reconciled, he had long been in the habit of paying me thus by slipping the check beneath my door, and therefore had always been planning to leave, as soon as the moment presented itself. So the money was not, then, intended for me, but indeed the elusive Tatiana, set to arrive *2/2/09*—which now I considered it was tomorrow—and whose contact information, which appeared to be local, appended the word-processed note. But who was she, this Tatiana, and what had the sub-leaser hired her to do? And why, furthermore, was her number a post-script as opposed to placed beside her name? When I added the numbers, successively, I arrived at the sum of 46. What did it signify, that number? Or was it merely happenstancial? And what, furthermore, had the sub-leaser meant when he thanked me, rather glibly, I thought, for the *shelter*? Did *shelter* refer to the shared space itself, in an easy and jocular way, perhaps, or did it have a more urgent, even literal dimension, as in *shelter from harm*, i.e., persecution, which put me in mind of nefarious doings that Hank might well have taken part in—ones that had driven him here, to these rooms, to seek respite in anonymity?

For what did I know about him, really, this trespasser into and out of my life? His name was Hank. His trade was law. His hair was close-shaved. His complexion was reddened. The checks that he wrote me never bounced. He lived alone inside the room. He was early to bed and early to rise. He hardly ever cooked.

In between prior tenants, I had not leased the room, though I could have with relative ease, I am sure, as the demand among students for similar rooms is great throughout the city where I live, which is expensive. But as I began to compose my thesis, I had less and less time to eke out pocket money, and my small fellowship had been cut by a third so as to provide for the less senior students who were just then beginning their coursework that fall. All of which resulted, in my fifth year of study, in my agreeing to host, for once, a sub-leaser, who had happened across my ad, he claimed, while reading the paper one morning at breakfast. I happened on the ad, he'd said, and it made good sense to inquire, so I did. Yet this, I should mention, at last, was impossible, for I had posted no such notice in the paper or elsewhere.

But here are some facts about the change, originating, as I mentioned, in the sub-leaser's room and extending its dominion northward. That room, the south room, was completely destroyed, so far as the word, destroyed, I mean, can be applied under proviso of a security deposit, which I should concede I had failed to draw up between the sub-leaser Hank and myself, upon move-in. There were two ragged fractures afflicting the baseboards that sit below the window-frames, one left and one right, in the room's southern wall where the windows themselves look out on the courtyard, and along the same stretch of the L, so described, that the windows of the living room look out on as well, this vista divided, inside the apartment, by a bisecting wall with a door centered in it.

The leftmost of these holes was large, running slant from the baseboard's northwest corner to where it met the wooden floor, while the rightmost hole, though just as dark, was smaller than the leftmost by nearly two-thirds, perpetrated one meter southeast of the first. Upon seeing the holes, I had knelt by the left one and put my eye against the void. The space within was parched and dusty, the air so still it seemed not air but a dark insulation in the walls, between the beams. A minuscule race of woodlice, maybe, crawled along the ridge of the hole, in the light. The rightmost hole, but a third of the leftmost, consisted of a corner where the plaster had buckled so as to show a gash of dark, as if a foot or a first had made it so, presumably that of the sub-leaser. I put my eye to this one, too, and a small sharp wind irritated my fluids.

I returned to the larger, leftmost hole and tested the air, which yet proved still, and then I returned to the rightmost again, where the tiny, sourceless draft still blew. Though the holes were strange and incoherent, they could have been due to some botched heavy lifting, perhaps the big desk that the sub-leaser worked at, positioned below, and between, the two windows, to enjoy what little cross-breeze had blown in from the courtyard.

Yet it was gone, the desk, I mean, along with every other article the room had contained. And the room itself an echo chamber, with a thick skirt of junk shoring in its four walls.

On the baseboards adjacent to those with the holes, beginning at the center of the room's western wall, there was a pale pinkish wax dribbled onto the plaster that trailed to the floor where it started to pool. An island chain of suchlike pools reached clear into the center of the room before fading. The widest of them looked so hard that I would doubtless have to face it with a chisel.

As for the junk at the base of the walls, it was banal as any junk. But just the same it struck me as a foul exaggeration of type of dorm-style living the apartment assumed. So many sweet wrappers, and beer bottle caps, and random receipts from habitual spending, and cigarette foils, and paper clips, and pennies, and nickels, and dimes, and some quarters, that it suggested that the person who had lived in the room, I had to assume the sub-leaser, had littered down along the walls in what appeared to be an even distribution.

In the northwest corner of the room, a pair of orthopedic shoes. White and with lifts, like the shoes of a nurse, or the shoes of a dead geriatric. One of the shoes lay slumped on its side, while the other of them sat upright, as if the owner had stood not a moment ago in the worn cushioning of the insole. The shoes were old and faintly dusty, with yellowed cloth tongues in place of shoelaces. It is also pertinent to note that both of the shoes were turned into the corner.

The forest-green pennant of some sports team still hung on the white of the wall, right of center.

Besides a few discolorations and dents in the wall, there was nothing else visibly changed in the room, which is not, in any way, to downplay the significance of the disparate holes, or the pools of dried wax, or the pair of orthopedic shoes, or the emptiness of the room itself, achieved in the space between two heartbeats, or what seemed, on reflection, to have been achieved thus in the five-hour period I'd been gone. Visibly changed, I specify, for I had not yet had occasion to open the closet, where I found, on a hanger tortured out of its shape, what remained of a cable-knit turtleneck sweater, stickily matted and infested with holes, as if it had been set aflame, doused with cold water, then set back to rights. On the floor of the closet, more random detritus, in what seemed to me a more or less uniform coating, and on top of which sat, in a maddening tangle, a series of plastic and copper coat-hangers.

I was just about to leave the closet when I chanced to hear a sifting sound, as of dirt being poured from some height to the floor, and I pushed aside the ruined sweater, hanging far left along the rack, to spy, in the closet's western corner, a dark obscuration, not part of the closet, suspended in the crevice where the walls met the ceiling. I stood on my toes to get a better look at it and prodded the shape a few times with my finger, which touched a little woven object, clung about with dirt. At the risk of fiddling with a light and startling the thing, which might yet be alive, I cupped my hand around the bottom and eased it away from the walls that retained it.

I held a desiccated bird's nest, with the mummified bits of a few dead chicks.

But barely recognizable as chicks, I should add, just as the bird's nest had been as a bird's nest. Shriveled knobs of black and brown, their dainty legs upcurled beneath them, flightless wings held fast and flush. There were four little avian corpses in all. I had never myself been one for pets. The bird's nest crumbled in my hand and into the cuff of the shirt I was wearing, collecting in the elbow, at the bend in the sleeve, where it sifted when I moved my arm.

I set the dead chicks on the bed of coat hangers, but left ajar the closet door.

The rest of the apartment beyond the south room was as I have described above. Which is to say no different concerning its contents, and the condition in which these things were kept, and the atmosphere surrounding these things, their surroundings—the character of the air, let's say—than they'd been when I left, hours ago, the apartment, to begin my daylong spate of errands. And yet they were different—were changed—were transformed—by the fact that they had been in the apartment when I hadn't, and might have borne witness to certain events gone on in the sub-leaser's room in my absence.

Promptly, I picked up my portable phone—the apartment does not have a landline—and dialed the local number with the sum of 46 that Hank, the sub-leaser, had included as a post-script. After several dry rings, a woman picked up, who had some sort of foreign accent, and through whom, by and by, it was revealed that the number belonged to a kind of maid service, which the woman with the accent who answered the phone assured was as professional, discreet and affordable as any I was likely to find in the city, and thusly would I find it said not only in the local papers, where the service in question had taken out ads, but in the countless testimonies of the service's patrons that I could consult if I wished confirmation. I thanked her, but no, she had been very helpful. I thanked her, but no, I was convinced.

But had I been, convinced, I mean, by the quality of service assured by the woman? Had it not been initially Hank, and not me, who had hired the maid service to see to the rooms he had left such a mess in his hasty departure and by that logic, might I say, that Hank alone had been convinced?

But Hank was nowhere and the service was coming, bearing down on the apartment like a messenger of doom. What could I do, marooned inside, but await, with a fortified mind, its arrival?

At the end of the call, I sat down on the couch, turning over the name of the maid Tatiana—Tatiana—Tatiana—ceaselessly, in my mind, while wondering, and you will, too, why I'd secured an outside party, when I was already in financial straits, to accomplish a chore that I could have accomplished with a minimum of time and effort; and one who, in good part, resembled the sub-leaser so far as she was unknown to me—or no better known to me, really, than

Hank, who himself had done little to recommend strangers. And when, to wit, this outside party, whose name was Tatiana, I must bear in mind, would possess very little to no context for the trials that I had suffered at the hands of the sub-leaser and might well think the south room mine, or at any rate exploited by me to such ends as the sub-leaser had had in mind.

Such ends, which were. Such ends, which were.

Suffice to say that they were ends.

Before dawn I was up, without much sleep, giving the apartment a cursory clean. I mopped the floors. I wiped the mirrors. I sponged across the counter-space. I even attacked the fussy toilet with a bristle-brush, a plunger and some squirts of blue slime. By the time I was done, a lemony smell overlaid the general staleness and my hands were chapped from working in the cold of the apartment, which I endured to save on gas. I walked nervously, critically, through the rooms, seeing my work through a stranger's eyes, and decided that this was the best I could do before the hour of one arrived.

The south room, however, I had not touched or rearranged in any way, with the logic that the room, manipulated in the slightest, would be able to deceive me when and if it changed again. The shoes with the lifts were turned into their corner. The wax abided on the boards. The decomposed birds lay scattered and brown on the bed of coat hangers on the floor of the closet.

Shortly after midday, the doorbell buzzed and an undefined voice came over the speakers. It was asking, I think, to be buzzed up, or asking me to say my name, but rather than do either thing, I said, Wait, and left for the first time in days the apartment, walking down eight flights of white marble stairs surmounted by a dark green banister, the same shade of green, it occurred to me, walking, as the pennant that hung on the sub-leaser's wall—who only several hours ago had taken a similar trip down the stairs, whilst all his possessions, including the desk, had amassed in a wordless cabal at the bottom.

Yet had the sub-leaser encountered this woman, who peered, curious, through a chink in her door?

This woman who looked old enough to wear the orthopedic shoes, not old enough to die in them, but old enough to wear them, surely, with ropes of grey hair, and a thin, collapsed mouth, and a posture that stiffened when I passed, the posture of a woman in misery. This woman watched me on my way, as if she'd never seen me in the building before, when in truth, I recalled in the moment I passed her, she had been my downstairs neighbor since I'd taken the room and had many times had the occasion to greet me, and had even received deliveries for me in the hours when I was not at home, so why did she look at me now like a stranger—as I had doubtless looked at her—and look at me, moreover, as she might well have looked at the dubious figure of Hank, the sub-leaser, dragging his possessions past her bend in the stairs, possibly in the dead of night, pausing just outside her door to gasp and readjust his weight.

I hurried to the bottom where a package waited for me, at the base of the stairs where the mailboxes were. But I saw no deliveryman, whose voice, I assumed, was the one I had heard, or had struggled to hear through the warp of the speaker. Not that it was so uncommon to be greeted with a parcel that did not require a signature, but that I'd expected to find Tatiana, the maid from the affordable, discrete cleaning service, and here was a package in her place, which struck me, obliquely, as somehow obscene, and I stood for a time, staring off into space, with the package extended in front of my abdomen. Stared for so long and with so little focus, that I almost did not see my name, written above the apartment's address, and over this central block of text a return address in smaller letters—yet clearly *my* return address, the same as the one written down for receiving, but missing my name, the designated recipient.

So I had been the sender and recipient both; or the sender, at least, by implication. What in the world, I tried hard to recall, could I have posted to myself?

The package was extremely light. I carried it up the flights of stairs and through the door of my apartment. When I locked, one by one, the door's two locks, I heard the echo of it in the landing outside.

In the kitchen I studied the package some more. It was hideously light for its size, which was considerable. The handwriting, I was glad to see, was not in the least similar to my own. Beginning in the corner, I cut through the cardboard and through the tape that held it fast, until one of the package's flaps popped loose to reveal a substratum of Styrofoam peanuts. I swept them from the frame of the box with such haste that they spilled, rudderless, to the floor of the kitchen, settling at last against the wall and beneath the slight ledge undergirding the sink. There was packaging paper beneath, several layers, with a couple orphaned bits of foam.

Under which—my hands trembled—there was nothing at all.

The package was a total void.

I set it on the countertop and sat, suddenly, on the floor of the kitchen. The window beside me admitted a draft that sent the foam peanuts wandering in all directions. I was dressed in my bathrobe and slippers, no more, and beneath the lapels of the robe, I felt clammy.

Such ends, which were. Such ends, which were. Who had sent the empty package? And whose handwriting, if not my own, had addressed it to these very rooms? The obvious answer was Hank, the sub-leaser, who had since abdicated his room, the south room, without the slightest explanation, hardly beyond the kind of prank that the self-addressed package entailed. But I had never got a look at the sub-leaser's writing, on account of the fact there was no lease, and therefore could not say for sure that his was the same as the kind on the package. Which admission, of course, is not to say that I didn't suspect him as the culprit, not just of addressing the package to me, but of bringing it here to the building himself, a thing he had done in record time, and then, more or less, in the following sequence: garbling his voice so as to disguise it; leaving the package by the stairs; fleeing the lobby, the block, the zip code at the risk of me making him out at his games, when even he knew, or must have known, that I would never pursue him beyond the last stair, for how many times had he passed by my room to find me so rapt at composing my thesis that I scarcely noticed him at all, much less decided to follow him?

175

Thus did he hold the clear advantage of knowing me better than I knew him. His name was Hank. His trade was law. He lived alone inside the room. He was early to bed and early to rise. He hardly ever cooked.

And who was the maid—this Tatiana? What did I really know of her? She sounded Eastern European, as had the woman on the phone. Which meant she might be in the country illegally, or indentured to a sex-trade racket, or else unacceptably underage, a waif of a girl in floral print dress, unless she was old, an old maid, so to speak, old enough to wear the shoes, older even than the woman on the stairs, my neighbor, who had not seemed to recognize me.

And what would she think either way, young or old?

What would be her diagnosis?

It was safe to say I knew her less than I had known the sub-leaser, for at least, with him, I'd seen his face, and could more or less predict his habits, and could venture a guess at his age, close to mine, though perhaps a couple years my junior.

And what would he think, the sub-leaser, if he entered the apartment at precisely this instant? What would he think had gone on in these rooms, the south room, the sub-leaser's room, in particular?

What kind of impression was I likely to make, having lived for so long under such poor conditions?

I was startled by the doorbell, buzzing. How long had I been on the floor of the kitchen? It could have been a minute, or an hour, or several hours, judging by the digits of the stove-clock, which were zeroes. I went down the hall, spoke into the buzzer and was met once again by the same garbled address, as if the buzzer were taking human speech and relaying it back to me in tongues. And I asked of the voice: Tatiana, is that you, as if I had known her all my life. She of the affordable, discrete cleaning service staffed by women from the Bloc. But I knew I could not buzz her up. The situation was larger than either of us, certainly larger than a cleaning, and what could I do but speak to this in the plainest terms that I could muster. Which is to say I did not speak. Which is to say I listened closely. There in the splintered, uncarpeted hall, between the front door and the room with the pipe.

By and by, the buzzing ceased, as did the incoherent words. The apartment, my apartment, was totally silent, and I slid down the wall to the floor.

But then came a knock. I drew up my knees. Clutching them, I listened and the knock came again. My name was spoken through the door, followed by a louder rap. Who's there, I called, and I was answered, Tatiana. Tatiana, said the voice. Clean, sir. I arrive. But what did she mean by that: *I arrive*, instead of, for instance, I am here, or, It is me, or, I *have* arrived, as would have been the proper English, her preferred choice of stating so simple a fact with such a grandiloquent verb as *arrive* giving her words a hint of menace, as if she were not of this world.

I pushed myself up against the wall. I peered through the circumscribed eye of the peephole. Not peering back but observing her shoes while flattening along her waist a dark and rather shapeless sweater was a short blonde woman with a paper shopping bag propped in the crook of her arm like an infant, and neither young nor old, this woman, there in the stairwell outside the apartment, or anyway not young or old in a way that was cause for concern or alarm. But not middle-aged. No, not that either. She was a woman in a sweater with a bag in her arms.

She knocked and said my name again, but still I stared and did not answer. I arrive, she repeated. You want come in? I could not think of what to say. She knocked again. You want come in? No, thank you, I managed to say in a voice that was too low to hear through the door. A look of irritation distorted her face. She gestured with her free right arm. I arrive, now I go, she said. I go. Which is exactly what I wanted her to do, so kept silent.

You pay, she said. You call. You pay. But I had no intention of paying, and I said so. I call, then, she said. *I* call. *You* pay. She seemed to be talking nonsense now. What did she mean that *she* would call? Was I, after all, not in the apartment, just beyond the bolted door, standing in the splintered hall not ten feet away from the room with the pipe, and the room with the pipe not twenty feet north of the subleaser's room with the dismantled shrine? Was it not my apartment that needed the cleaning, as opposed to her apartment, wherever it was? What did she mean? What did anything mean? What had we come to, she and I?She set the bag between her feet, drew a phone out of her pocket and was soon engaged in dialing with her thumb on the keypad, waiting for her call to place, seeking the voice of someone, maybe, to help her navigate my treachery.

And then I watched her hang up the phone, Tatiana, squeeze it shut like a sort of castanet, as a thin fold of bills, which was really three twenties, emerged at her feet through the crack in the door.

She smiled, reached down, took the money and left.

What had possessed me to pay? With what money?

My prospects were now completely barren.

The service had been indiscreet, I decided. Not to mention unaffordable.

But had it been unprofessional? Did it deserve to be stripped of that title? Had Tatiana not been courteous, only attacking when faced with resistance? And were I her, confronting me, would I not have done the same?

But since I was not—that is, Tatiana—I could not presume to know her thoughts. I could only say what I would do, which marked the extent of our fellowship.

Such ends, which were. Alone again. I wandered down the splintered hall.

Past the bathroom, the kitchen, the room with the pipe, otherwise known as the north room, my room, and thence into the living room where no one, not even myself, had sat, and finally into the subleaser's room, with the sibilant hole and the mute one beside it, and the shoes with the lifts turned into the corner as if I had rebuked them there, and the pools of pink wax, dried so long ago, and the four dead birds—what kind?—in the closet.

Both of the shades were drawn on the windows, while the windows themselves were very clean. The sub-leaser, if nothing else, had thought to take care of these windows.

Outside was the courtyard and beyond it other buildings, where people like me went to bed and woke up, and where there were probably other sub-leasers living in similar types of rooms. Official sub-leasers under written contracts, and ones where the contracts were implied, and believe it or not, less official ones still, who paid for the rooms where they lived by the week, or who slept on the living room couch, passing through, without being asked to pay at all, though likely as not these latter ones were guests of the primary tenants. They were not, that I knew of, bad people, or dangerous in any way, but there, between the courtyard of my building and the next, mounted on a ledge of concrete, was a chain-link fence about ten feet strung along with razor-wire, running to points both east and west of the dark alleyway in between the blocks of buildings. And it was this, the razor-wire, as opposed to the fence, that I had never noticed in my five years as a tenant, but that I now appreciated in a visceral way, in the way that one appreciates death and things of it.

What was the fence keeping out of the building?

Or what was the fence keeping in, on my side?

Who was Tatiana, and where the sub-leaser?

Who would I lease the room to now?

Acknowledgments

So many thanks you's and so little space. But I'll try.

Thank you, reader, for picking this up. Thank you to my classmates and teachers in Columbia University's MFA Program for book-talk, encouragement and not pulling punches: Lincoln Michel, James Yeh, Adam Wilson, Emily Cooke, Selena Anderson, Jess Sauer, Caroline Seklir, Annie DeWitt, Dave Varno, Jay Deshpande, Rebecca Curtis, Joshua Furst and Jaime Manrique. And special thanks to both Christine Schutt and Heidi Julavits, who helped to refine and delouse many of these stories at various crucial stages in their development. A colossal, world-swallowing thank you to Ben Marcus, who has done and continues to do so much for me on so many fronts—you're a friend and a mentor. Thank you to John Wray for the words, and for not having me arrested as I've worshipfully kept in touch over the years. Thank you to the Pauls of Vassar College (Kane & Russell) who first helped me find my sea legs in this perilous business. Thank you to the Henfield-Transatlantic Foundation, and to Binnie Kirshenbaum for affording me time, via money, to produce. Thank you to Diane Goettel and Angela Leroux-Lindsey for believing in me, and to the rest of the Black Lawrence Press/Dzanc Books family, with special shout-outs to Patrick Michael Finn and Adam Prince. Thank you to my students at BB&N and Grub Street for allowing me, in glimpses, to see the world outside. And thank you, as well, to the Grub Street crew for faith, advice, community. Thank you to Rebecca Maslen for designing a rad cover. Thank you to Raegan McCain and Steven

Brykman at Got Your Nose for designing a rad website. Thank you to Annie Laurie Erickson and Sean Flynn for taking a rad picture. Thank you to Betsy Groban for publishing know-how and support. Thank you to the many friends out there who have helped me to hoist, in various ways, the banner of authorship: Aaron Pores, James Griffin, Jeff McLamb, Jefferson Grau, Andrea O'Meara, Jane Gregory, Molly Boyle and too many Boston, New York and San Diego friends to here name—you are unmatched. Thank you to my one-of-a-kind grandma Elaine, and sister Marin, and to the rest of the Milstein-Van Young clan, and the Roake/Checks (J. Michael, Jo Anne, Jessica, Dan, Elliot and Sylvie)—your collective support means the world to me. Illimitable thanks to my mom, Marjorie Milstein, and my dad, Eric Van Young, for always believing in their hearts that their son could become a writer, and for bringing that belief to bear in their daily lives. And thank you forever and always to my wife and my snow leopard, Darcy Roake, without whom I wouldn't be much, well, at all.